Mystery In Time

Deborah Edmisten

**Cover Art By
Michelle Mulligan**

*For Charlie ~
My best friend*

IN BOOK ONE...

In the first book of the *In Time* series, twelve-year-old

Emarie Gordon discovers an antique typewriter in her friend,

Glenda's, antique shop in Killbuck, Ohio. The typewriter

mysteriously opens a time traveling portal and carries Emarie back

in time to 1901. After arriving in 1901, Emarie meets Victoria and

Emmeline Hill, the teenage daughters of the wallpaper

manufacturing tycoon, Brandon Hill, and his wife Eva. She also

meets their ten-year-old scullery maid, Lorna James, and their teen

stable hand, Stefan Cano.

After Emarie convinces her new friends that she is indeed

from the future by predicting the assassination of President William

McKinley, they go in search of an Underwood No. 5 typewriter,

hoping that using an exact replica of the typewriter that sent Emarie to 1901 will somehow transport her back home to the year 2018.

Along the way, they experience many adventures – fighting off thieves who try to rob their carriage, rescuing a boy named Robert from an orphan train, and tangling with a villain named Conrad Beesly. As the story closes, they discover an Underwood No. 5 typewriter that sends Emarie back to her own time.

After Emarie is transported back to 2018 and wakes up in the antique shop, she realizes that her time in 1901 was truly real and not a dream. Glenda, who has no idea that Emarie has traveled through time, tells Emarie to go home and rest, worried that she may be sick because she's acting so strangely. Emarie heads toward home, thrilled with the knowledge that she has actually traveled through time. And this is where our new adventure begins…

CHAPTER ONE

Emarie made her way past all the shops and buildings on Front Street and onto the lane that led home. She twirled and whirled and danced and laughed her way up the lane, overwhelmed with the wonder of all she'd experienced. Just when she thought her heart couldn't stand more happiness, she froze in place, arrested by the sight of four figures at the top of the hill by her home.

They were standing under the huge willow tree, waving to her from the distance. Two were clothed in beautiful bright dresses, and the third, in the uniform of a scullery maid. The fourth – a young man dressed for stable work, shielded his eyes from the brilliant sunlight. "What?" Emarie whispered in disbelief, slowly inching forward. "How?"

"Emarie! Emarie! It's us!" a female voice called loudly. Emarie instantly recognized it as Victoria's as her words were

carried by the wind down the hill to where Emarie stood. With that,

the four figures rushed toward her as one, the hems of the girls' long

dresses brushing across the lush green grass of Emarie's backyard.

As they moved closer, Emarie's heart nearly burst with

happiness. How it could be she didn't know – that it was real was

all that truly mattered now. She raced to them as fast as her feet

would carry her, her arms open wide.

They met halfway up the hill, the girls gathering one another

into a crushing embrace, crying for joy. Stefan looked on, grinning

from ear-to-ear. When Emarie couldn't wait one second longer to

ask them how they'd gotten to her time, she pulled away from their

embrace and hugged Victoria, Emmeline and Lorna one by one,

laughing and crying at the same time. They ended up in a circle as

Stefan stepped in to join them, their faces wet with tears.

"How? How did you get here?!" Emarie asked excitedly, her

words tinged with awe as she looked at each one of them in

amazement, her eyes hungrily taking in every detail of their

tearstained faces.

"Oh, my goodness! It was astounding! I've never

experienced anything like it in my life!" Lorna shrieked, throwing up her hands in exhilaration as they all laughed aloud at her excitement.

"It still boggles my mind!" Victoria exclaimed. "We're here with you! *But how can it be*?!"

"Did you get here through the typewriter?" Emarie asked in a rush, eager for answers. "I just got back here to my own time only fifteen minutes ago…how did you manage to arrive here on the exact day and almost the exact same time that I got back from 1901?"

"Yes, the typewriter brought us here! We had no control over it…we didn't know it was going to send us here to you! We were as shocked to see you just now as you were to see us!" Emmeline responded excitedly.

"And it's 1902 in our time now!" Lorna exclaimed. Emarie shook her head, completely bewildered.

"We were surprised to see you, but we have been talking a lot about time travel since you left us, and we may have an idea about why we were brought here to you," Stefan said, his gaze intensely serious as the mood among them changed dramatically. Emarie sensed the shift but didn't understand it. "Do you recall that our faces were in the clouds right before you were sent back to your time?" he asked. Emarie nodded slowly, confused about the somber mood that had suddenly fallen over them.

Emmeline abruptly interrupted Stefan, words pouring out of her like an unstoppable flood. "Do you remember how you said you believed you were sent to 1901 to save Robert…that he was the reason you were there? Well, we talked endlessly about that after you were sent back to your time, and we absolutely agreed…you saw visions from 1901 in the clouds before the portal opened in 2018 and sent you to our time, and that meant your mission was to save Robert. We became convinced that when a person sees visions from another time…or sees themselves in the clouds…that it means they have a mission to complete somewhere in time. We tried over and over to open the portal using the Underwood, certain that we had a mission to complete since we'd seen our faces in the cloud…but nothing ever happened…we were never transported anywhere. We couldn't understand why the portal never opened when we felt absolutely certain that the vision we'd seen the day you left had to mean something. But then a dreadful event occurred with Father, and we urgently needed help, so we tried the typewriter once again out of desperation, hoping and praying that it would take us to the past so we could find answers…and it *worked*…but we weren't transported to the past…we were brought *here*…to *you*…in *your time*!" Emmeline finished breathlessly.

"This is unbelievable!" Emarie gasped. "But what dreadful thing happened to your Father?" she asked, her mind whirling as her heart filled with dread.

"He's been accused of a terrible crime!" Victoria cried, wringing her hands.

"What?!" Emarie gasped in disbelief. "What has he been accused of?"

"Attacking a guard at his company and leaving him for dead!" Lorna sobbed, hot tears falling onto her cheeks.

Emarie stared at them in stunned disbelief, unable to comprehend the horror of the words they'd uttered. "It can't be," she finally said in a hushed whisper.

"No, you're correct, it *can't* be," Stefan emphatically agreed in his Albanian-accented English. "That must be why we've been sent here! For some reason, you must be the key to saving Mr. Hill."

Emarie shook her head, completely confused. "But why would you be sent to 2018 because of a crime committed in 1902?"

she questioned, holding her suddenly aching head. "Like I told you, I just returned to my time fifteen minutes ago...why would the typewriter have brought you here looking for answers? I'm so confused!"

"There *must* be an answer here in your time!" Victoria insisted. "I can't see how there's any other explanation."

"We have to save Father!" Emmeline cried. "The man who was attacked is in a coma, and if he dies and father is convicted of killing him, he could hang!"

"Hang?" Emarie gasped, her hand flying to her mouth in shock.

"I'm afraid so," Stefan said somberly. "In our time, they act very decisively against such a crime. He would hang within days after a conviction."

"But surely the evidence will show that he's innocent?" Emarie responded, her anguished words hanging in the air as they looked at her in silence, their faces lined with pain.

After several moments, Victoria found the composure to speak. "The evidence against him is overwhelming. It truly looks as if Father attacked the guard for trying to steal from the retail shop."

"No! No, no, no! Please don't say that!" Emarie cried.

"We know it's not true, but someone has gone to great pains to make it look as if he committed the crime. Someone has framed him for the attack," Stefan responded.

"Framed him? Who would want to do such a thing?! He's a good and kind man!"

"We don't know, but we're desperate to uncover the truth!" Emmeline cried.

Emarie looked at them, her heart pounding in her chest. "How can I possibly help you? What can I possibly do to save your father?" she whispered, tears nearly closing her throat.

As they stood together, speechless in their pain, a faint voice could be heard calling in the distance. "Emarie! Emarie! Are you out there? It's time to eat!"

Emarie stiffened in alarm, her panicked eyes darting toward her house at the top of the hill, then back to her four desperate friends. "Oh, no! It's my mom! I need to hide you! Come on!"

CHAPTER TWO

"I'll be there in a few minutes, Mom!" Emarie yelled, silently motioning to Stefan and the girls to follow her. Emarie hurriedly led them the rest of the way down the hill and then onto a trail than ran through a patch of woods on the property line of her home. The sun shone through the spaces between the canopy of leaves overhead, dancing softly around their feet as they made their way deeper into the trees. Finally, Emarie stopped before a tall and sturdy oak tree. She pointed to the top of the tree, a smile lining her face. "My treehouse," she said, struggling to catch her breath. "You can hide here until I get back. I'll try to hurry."

"It's amazing!" Stefan said, eyeing the elaborate treehouse sitting high in the branches of the aged oak. They all looked up, their faces creased with admiration. The house was sided with wood scallops painted a delicate pale blue and its windows were lined with real glass panes, graced on either side by white shutters. There were tiny white flower boxes beneath the windows, filled with bright flowers spilling over the sides. The faux chimney was made of real stone and the roof was covered with individual white wood shingles. "I've never seen anything quite like it," Stefan said admiringly.

"It's gorgeous!" Emmeline agreed, while Victoria and Lorna nodded their silent appreciation, smiling.

"My dad's an amazing carpenter!" Emarie responded. "He always wanted a treehouse when he was a little and he was never able to have one, so he kind of went a little crazy with mine...but a good crazy," she laughed.

"Emarie!" a voice called, still faint, but drawing closer to where the five of them stood.

"Hurry! Go up! It's my mom looking for me!" Emarie urged, gently pushing Lorna toward the tree.

"How are we going to make it up wearing our gowns?" Victoria whispered urgently, eyeing the narrow slats nailed to the massive oak tree.

"Do your best," Emarie whispered. "I'm going to try and distract her. I'll be back as soon as I can!" With those parting words, Emarie took off running full speed toward the sound of her mother's voice. She was driven partly by fear of the girls and Stefan being discovered, but more so by the desire to see her mom's face. To her mother, she'd only been gone for an hour, but to Emarie, it had been weeks on end. She came up just short of her mom on the trail and threw her arms around her, hugging her with all her might.

Marci Gordon laughed, hugging Emarie tightly in return. "What's this all about? You're acting like you haven't seen me for weeks!"

It took every ounce of self-control Emarie had not to shout, *It has been weeks! I've missed you so much!* "I just love you," she said instead, stroking her mom's hair, breathing in the smell of her – the smell of the person who had cared for and loved her since the day she was born. She had desperately missed her parents and it felt wonderful to see and touch her mom again.

"Well, that's nice to know!" her mom laughed again, squeezing Emarie one last time before releasing her. "So, any new interesting antique finds at Arnold's?" she asked, eyeing Emarie quizzically.

For the second time in a matter of seconds, Emarie had to

bite her tongue. What would her mom say if she told her that she'd found an antique Underwood No. 5 typewriter that had transported her back in time to 1901? What would she say if she told her that she'd been part of completing a mission that had reunited a little boy with his parents after almost being torn from them for life? What would her mom say if she told her that some of the people she'd met in 1901 were now hiding in her treehouse? She smiled instead, choosing her words carefully. "Glenda found an amazing Underwood No. 5 typewriter from the turn of the century and it looks almost brand new!"

"Whoa, awesome!" her mom responded enthusiastically. Marci was genuinely excited. Every bit of the love Emarie had for the olden days was the direct result of Marci passing her love for history on to Emarie. Since the time Emarie was old enough to walk, Marci had taken her daughter with her on tours of historical homes, bought her old-fashioned paper dolls, taken her to historical villages and antique stores, and had even taken Emarie along while she traveled Underground Railroad routes.

"It's amazing!" Emarie said, nearly jumping up and down, flashes of memory coursing through her mind…the Hill's and their guests dancing as she watched through the open French doors, the thieves trying to rob their carriage and Victoria beating one of them over the head with her parasol, saving Robert from the orphan train, Gabardine Fusk flying through the air and landing in a heap at her feet, Senora Sierra destroying the warehouse door with an axe, taking Conrad Beesly down…it all rushed through her mind in a flurry of beloved remembrance.

"Why don't you take me to see it after dinner?" Marci asked, finding Emarie's exuberance contagious.

"Ummm…well…" Emarie faltered, suddenly realizing what could happen if her mom touched the typewriter keys. To see her mom carried away to another time right before her eyes would be more than Emarie could bear. "Well, I think Glenda m-might be closing the store soon," Emarie fibbed, hoping her mom wouldn't detect the stutter that almost always appeared when she was being less than honest.

Marci Gordon narrowed her eyes, examining Emarie's face carefully. "Really? I thought she was open until 7:00 tonight?"

"Ummm…I don't think she's feeling well," Emarie said hurriedly without stuttering.

"Oh, okay. Well, maybe we can walk over tomorrow and see it if she's feeling better. I'm also itching to see if she has any new antique world globes."

Emarie breathed a sigh of relief as her mom seemed to accept her explanation of Glenda not feeling well. She chuckled at her mom. "Don't you have enough globes, Mom? A new one would make, what…thirty?"

"Hey, you can never have too much of a good thing," Marci countered, playfully poking Emarie in the side.

Emarie laughed and retreated out of the reach of her mom's hand after the jab. "Dad's going to harass you, you know that, right?"

"He's a fine one to talk! He has about sixty model cars! If he gets on me about my globes, I'll just sweetly remind him about his *shelves* of cars," Marci winked.

"Oh, yeah, sweetly…I'm sure," Emarie giggled.

"Hey, watch it!" Marci laughed in response. "By the way," she said, suddenly changing the subject. "I have some new things for your kitchen," she added, turning slightly to show Emarie a backpack attached to her shoulders. "Why don't we go put them up in your treehouse before supper?"

Emarie's heart began to frantically race in her chest. Her mind screamed *Stop!* but she struggled desperately to keep her expression from looking startled. What could she say to distract her mom? How could she keep her away from the treehouse? "Mom, I'm starving! I'll just take the backpack and set it by the tree, then I'll unpack it after supper."

"It'll just take a few minutes," her mom countered. "Let's just do it now and get it out of the way. I don't want any animals to get into it while we're eating."

And with that, Marci Gordon headed down the path toward the treehouse, chattering about antique globes and how beautiful they are as Emarie trailed behind her, trying to come up with a legitimate reason to keep her mom out of the treehouse. She was growing more and more panicked as her mom approached the base of the tree and then put her foot on the first step on the old oak. "Mom! No!" Emarie screamed, her dark eyes crazed with fear.

CHAPTER THREE

"Emarie, what in the world is wrong with you? Why are you screaming at me?" Marci yelled back at her daughter, completely flustered.

"I – I – I…I thought I saw something," Emarie stuttered.

"Why are you stuttering? Is there something in the treehouse you don't want me to see?" Marci asked, her eyes narrowing again as she examined Emarie's flushed cheeks. "That's not like you, Emarie. What's going on?"

"N-nothing," Emarie stuttered again, on the verge of tears.

"Okay, now I'm going up for sure. What in the world?" she muttered as she slowly made her way up the wooden slats to the treehouse.

Emarie danced in nervous circles, panicking. How was she going to explain Stefan and the girls to her mom? She would think she'd lost her mind if she told her they were time travelers. Could she say they were all practicing for a play? That she'd been asked to play a child in the cast of the high school production of some olden days play? No, it was too early in the school year for that. *Ahhh! What was she going to do?!* She waited in dread for her mom to reappear.

Moments later, Marci poked her head out of the treehouse door, her expression clearly perplexed. "Emarie, what is going on? There's nothing up here. Why are you acting so strange?"

Emarie stood frozen in place, stunned. *They weren't in the treehouse?! Where were they?!* She looked to her left and to her right, her eyes darting back and forth, scanning every inch of the nearby trees. She didn't see them anywhere. *Where could they be?!*

"Emarie!" her mom insisted. "What is going *on*? You look scared to death!"

Emarie swallowed hard, trying to steady herself. She knew if she stuttered, her mom wouldn't give up trying to figure out what was wrong. She swallowed again and licked her dry lips. "I'm working on a surprise," she said evenly without faltering. "Come down or you're going to ruin it," she said, realizing the ironic truth in her words.

Marci laughed as realization dawned. "Oh, a *surprise!* I'm so dumb!" she exclaimed, quickly scampering back down the wooden steps. "You could have just said you were working on a surprise!"

"Then the surprise would have been ruined…which it kind of is now," Emarie responded as her mom stopped in front of her, feeling herself blush as the lie became more complex.

"Oh, it's not," Marci said, kissing her cheek. "I have no idea what you're up to, so I'll still be surprised," she reassured. "Come on, let's go eat, and you can get back to your surprise after supper," she soothed, tucking her arm into Emarie's.

Emarie smiled at her mom, then subtly stole a glance behind her, trying again to spot Stefan and the girls. They were nowhere in sight. She prayed that her mom wouldn't be able to feel the thunderous pounding of her heart as they walked arm in arm. Where could they have gone? Were they hiding somewhere? Had they been carried back to their own time? Was it even possible for that to happen without the Underwood? Emarie's mind whirled in confusion as she attempted to act completely normal with her mom.

Side by side, they made their way up the rolling hill in front of their turn of the century home and walked into the mudroom where Emarie's dad bent over, taking off his boots after a long day at work. Emarie instantly threw her arms around him, crushing him with the strength of her embrace. Brian Gordon laughed heartily, squeezing his daughter in return. "What did I do to deserve such an epic hug?" he chuckled.

"She gave me that same bear hug just a few minutes ago," her mom interjected, smiling. "She's either up to no good, or she wants something," Marci joked, tugging playfully on Emarie's dark hair.

"I just love you both so much," Emarie said softly, her throat thick with emotion. If they only knew all that she'd been through in 1901 and how desperately she'd missed them. But how could she tell them such a thing? What adult would ever believe in something like time travel?

"Well, you may not want anything, but I have something for you," Brian said, giving Emarie another tight squeeze before disengaging from her hug. He grabbed an envelope from the counter beside the mudroom sink and handed it to her. "This came in the mail for you today."

Emarie took it, curious. She never got mail. Her mom looked over her shoulder, reading the name written in the return address section of the envelope. "Dezirae Carson. I don't know anyone by that name. Do you?" Marci questioned.

"Oh, that's my new pen pal!" Emarie exclaimed. "We were assigned pen pals from a school in Akron at the beginning of the year. We're supposed to write letters to each other the old-fashioned way all during the school year and then at the end of the year, we're going to meet each other at a party."

"That's really neat! That will be fun!" her dad responded. "Do you find it amusing that our daughter refers to handwritten letters as writing the 'old-fashioned way?'" he asked Marci, chuckling. "What's this world coming to?"

"Well, she's growing up in a world very different from the world we grew up in and we grew up in a world very different from the world our parents grew up in. Time and progress march on, my dear. You're just going to have to get used to it," Marci smiled.

As Brian groaned, Emarie headed toward the back-kitchen stairs that led to the hallway on the second floor of her home. "I'm going to go read my letter," she said, her panicked mind racing as she pictured the girls and Stefan alone and confused.

"Don't be long…supper's almost ready," her mom called after her.

Emarie ran up the steps two at a time, racing toward her bedroom. She burst through the door, then closed and locked it behind her. She paced around the room, trying to figure out what she should do next. If she didn't eat supper with her parents, they would be suspicious. She had to get through supper before going back to the treehouse. But then what? Where were they? Could the typewriter have brought them all to her time only to yank them back again? Why had they been sent to 2018? Just to see her? Emarie felt certain there had to be more to it than that, but she had no idea what it could be.

She sighed heavily, looking down at the wrinkled envelope she still held in her clenched fist. She shrugged. She might as well pass the time until she could get back to them. She tore open the envelope and pulled out the single sheet of lined paper folded into three. She carefully unfolded it and began reading:

Dear Emarie,

Hi! My name is Dezirae Carson and I live in Akron. But you already know that. How are things in Killbuck? I can't even imagine living in the country like you do. I've lived in the city my whole life. But I'd love to live in the country. Do you have animals? Like cows and pigs? I wonder if everyone in the country has cows and pigs? Do you have chickens? Do you have any brothers or sisters? I have three brothers and one sister. They're all older than me. Sometimes it stinks being the baby of the family. Everyone is always telling you what to do or to get stuff for them. All. Of. The. Time. If you do have brothers or sisters, I hope you're the oldest!

I live in a duplex with my family near downtown Akron. It's crowded, but we all fit. Did you know that Lebron James grew up in Akron? Do you know who he is? He's a great basketball player in the NBA! There are some neat places in Akron. My favorite place is called Stan Hywet. It's an old mansion that was built by one of the men who founded Goodyear. Do you know what Goodyear is? It's a company that make tires. Anyway, Stan Hywet is AMAZING! It's one of the biggest homes in the United States! We went there on a field trip last year and I can't stop thinking about it. The house was finished in 1915. It's so cool with all of the old-fashioned furniture and clothes the family used to wear. I love old-fashioned stuff! Do you? Wouldn't it be so cool if we could go back in time and live like people did in the olden days?

A huge smile spread across Emarie's face. If Dezirae only knew how cool it actually was!

CHAPTER FOUR

Twenty minutes later, after eating the quickest meal of her life, Emarie ran from the house like her feet were on fire. She made her way into the patch of woods along the property line and down the trail that led to her treehouse. She arrived at the treehouse breathless, frantically calling out as loud as she dared. "Victoria! Emmeline! Stefan! Lorna! Where are you?"

Within moments, she heard the rustling of leaves and the four confused time travelers slowly emerged from a thick of trees, waving to Emarie. Lorna had her hand over her mouth, fighting back laughter at the sight of Emarie's panicked face. "Here we are!" Victoria called.

"I'm so sorry," Emarie responded, rushing to them. "Are you okay? You scared me to death! I thought for sure that you were up in the treehouse and my mom was going to find you!"

"We're just fine," Emmeline said, reassuring her.

"There was no way we could all get up in time with your mother as close as she was," Stefan interjected. "So, we made a run for the trees."

"That was a smart idea!" Emarie responded. "I still can't believe you're here!" she added, a huge smile erupting as the fact that she was standing face to face with them hit home once again. "It's simply amazing!"

"And you're back in your time, where wearing your underclothes is acceptable," Lorna giggled, pointing at Emarie's shorts and t-shirt. The two of them laughed as they recalled Lorna asking Emarie why she was wandering about in her underclothes after Lorna had discovered her in the Hill's kitchen back in 1901.

Victoria interrupted their laughter, her words tinged with frightened urgency. "Emarie, we're so very happy to see you again. I can't begin to tell you how much...but we have to act quickly to help father! I can't bear the thought of him sitting in prison, knowing he could possibly hang for a crime he did *not* commit!" Stefan and Emmeline nodded silently in agreement, their faces darkened by anxiety.

Emarie and Lorna immediately sobered as Victoria's words reminded them of the fate that awaited Brandon Hill unless they could succeed in helping him. "You're right. But let's get up into the treehouse first before anyone sees us," Emarie urged, signaling them to follow her as she rushed toward the oak tree. She began climbing up the steps with the others following closely behind her. After Emarie made it up, she watched from the treehouse doorway as the girls carefully managed the precarious climb up the wood slats, struggling with their long dresses the whole way up. Stefan did his best to assist them, then quickly ambled up after all the girls had made it safely inside. They sat together in a circle in front of the false fireplace on the plush blue carpet lining the treehouse floor, ready to begin their search for answers.

"As we said earlier, there must be some reason the typewriter sent us here to you, Emarie. There has to be something that only you could help us with before it's too late for Mr. Hill," Stefan said.

Emarie chewed her lower lip, thinking. "I truly don't know what that could be. I'm twelve years old. How could I do anything to help save Mr. Hill? Think, think, think," she commanded herself. Several minutes went by as Emarie wracked her brain while the others sat watching her, helpless. The despair in the treehouse grew stronger with each passing moment of silence. At last, Emarie's eyes finally shined with the hint of a possibility. "Information!" she shouted.

"Information?" Victoria questioned, looking at her doubtfully.

"The Internet! It can tell you anything! We need to look at what happened with the investigation into the attack…and find out if the guard actually dies…what happens! If we can find out what happened in 1902, looking back from here in the future, maybe we'll be able to find a way to clear your father of attacking that man in your time!"

"What is the Inter…net?" Lorna asked hesitantly, her words tinged with suspicion.

Emarie thought, searching for the best words to describe something they would have no ability to comprehend. "It's like all the books in the world being available to read when you type on something like a typewriter…it's called a computer."

"My head is spinning," Emmeline moaned, her gloved hand resting on her temple.

"Where will we be able to find one of these...compters?" Stefan asked, stumbling over the unknown word.

"Not compter...com-pu-ter," Emarie answered slowly. "We have several computers at my house...but I can't take you there...how would I explain you to my mom and dad? There are also computers at the library in town, but I can't take you there dressed the way you are. The first thing I need to do is get you some clothes! Clothes that will help you blend in here in 2018."

"Shorts and a t-shirt?" Lorna giggled, her heart racing at the idea of wearing so little clothing.

"Where will you get so many clothes at such short notice? Won't it cost a great deal of money?" Emmeline questioned.

"There's a thrift shop in town," Emarie answered, noticing their questioning looks after she mentioned the shop. "It's a place where you buy used clothing."

"*Used* clothing?" Victoria asked, aghast. "People buy clothes that perfect strangers have worn?"

"Pretty much," Emarie laughed.

Emmeline wrinkled her nose in disgust but fought back her natural distaste for something so foreign to someone of her social station in 1902. "We'll do anything we need to do to blend in. Our mission is to save father and we'll do whatever it takes."

"Okay, great!" Emarie answered. "I'll need the sizes you wear so I don't buy something too large or too small."

"Sizes?" Victoria questioned, confused.

"Yes. Do you wear a size six or around an eight? Lorna would probably wear a children's size ten."

"I'm so confused," Emmeline responded. "I don't know anything about sizes. Our clothes are made for us by Mrs. Fusk and her seamstresses."

"Good 'ol Gabardine Fusk," Emarie laughed. "There's no one quite like her!" The others laughed along, the girls once again picturing Gabardine Fusk flying through the air in the Pullman car and landing in a dazed heap on the floor.

"Please, if you can find me some trousers instead of shorts, I would appreciate that. I can't imagine having my legs exposed," Stefan interjected after their giggles had subsided. He blushed slightly, embarrassed.

"I will," Emarie smiled. "I'll do my best to find dresses for all of you," she said to the girls. "They'll be shorter than you're used to, but it won't be such a drastic change as wearing shorts would be."

Victoria's chin went up, a look of defiance in her eyes. "I don't need a dress. A pair of trousers or shorts will work for me. If I'm going to be a young lady from 2018, I want to experience it to the fullest!"

"Oh, Victoria!" Emmeline groaned. "You always have to be scandalous!"

"I want to be scandalous, too!" Lorna chimed in, not willing to be left out of the experience.

Emarie shook her head, chuckling again. "You all are going to give me fits, I can tell that already. Okay, I'll be back soon. Whatever you do, don't leave this treehouse!"

"Can you bring us back some food?" Emmeline asked, holding her stomach. "I'm famished!" The others nodded emphatically in agreement.

"Oh, my gosh!" Emarie said. "I'm so sorry! I was in such a rush to get back to you, I didn't even think about food. I was starving when I exited the portal into your time – you have to be starving, too! I'll get back as fast as I can!"

With those parting words, Emarie headed toward the door of the treehouse, pausing just as her hand made contact with the doorknob. A thought suddenly occurred to her and she turned to her friends excitedly, her face glowing with elation. "Wait! You're going to fit in perfectly in those clothes for tomorrow at least! Killbuck's Early American Days festival is tomorrow and the next day! A lot of people will be dressed up like the olden days! No one will ever suspect that you're from 1902!"

CHAPTER FIVE

Emarie hummed to herself as she made her way down the sidewalk on Front Street. The thought of what might await Brandon Hill upset her immensely – but seeing her friends again had filled her heart with joy despite the fear she had for Mr. Hill. Technically, she hadn't been apart from them long at all, but the sorrow of leaving 1901 without knowing if she'd ever see them again had been devastating – and now that sadness was behind her.

She climbed the steps to the Pizza Parlor restaurant and swung the door open, closing her eyes and inhaling the delicious smells of the restaurant as she walked in. A few of the tables were occupied with people chatting as they ate their pizzas. The juke box played softly in the background, rounding out the pleasant atmosphere of the eatery. Emarie went to the smaller section at the back of the restaurant that was used for carry-out orders and waited at the bar.

Tracy Beecher came out of the kitchen, the door swinging behind her as she took her place behind the bar top, smiling at Emarie. "Want something to eat, Kiddo?" she asked, grabbing an order pad and pen from under the bar.

"Can I get a large pepperoni pizza and four Coke's to go?" she asked.

"Sure! That it?"

"Yep! Thanks! I'll be over at the thrift store...I'll pick it up on my way back," Emarie responded. Tracy waved as Emarie left through the side door of the restaurant.

Emarie walked the few yards to the thrift store, waving to the woman behind the checkout counter as she walked in. "Hey, Miss Jan!"

"Hey, Emarie! What're you up to today?"

"Ummm," Emarie stumbled, suddenly realizing that she didn't have a cover story if anyone asked why she was buying so many clothes. "Ummm...looking for some clothes for an orphanage in Ghana that our church is helping," she responded, feeling very uneasy with the lie.

"Oh, that's nice of you!" Jan Mulligan responded. "Let me know if you need any help finding anything."

"Okay, I will," Emarie answered, feeling the prick of her conscience as she rushed to the clothing room at the back of the store.

She stood before the racks of clothes feeling overwhelmed, wondering where to begin when she didn't even know sizes for the girls and Stefan. Lorna would be easy since Emarie had just recently been in Lorna's size herself, but Victoria and Emmeline, and especially Stefan, were going to be a challenge. She took a deep breath and headed toward the children's section, deciding to start her clothing search for Lorna first. After ten minutes of rummaging for a dress and coming up with nothing, she decided on a pair of red overall shorts and a red and white flowered t-shirt to go with them. It wasn't the ideal pick, but Emarie giggled, knowing that Lorna would relish the experience of wearing shorts in the world of 2018.

Thirty minutes later, a small mound of clothing lay at her feet. In addition to Lorna's overall shorts, denim shorts and a lilac t-shirt for Victoria now lay in the pile – as well as a pink sundress for Emmeline, and jeans and a blue Tommy Hilfiger t-shirt for Stefan.

Emarie scratched her head as she thought about shoes. Emmeline and Stefan's shoes would work with the clothes she'd picked out – and probably Lorna's – but Victoria was going to look ridiculous wearing lace-up dress boots with shorts and a t-shirt. The thought made Emarie laugh out loud and once the laughter took hold, she couldn't stop. She leaned against one of the racks to steady herself as she laughed until she cried, tears pouring down her face.

"What's so funny?" she heard an instantly recognizable voice ask. Emarie froze, the laugh dying in her throat as Glenda looked at her curiously. She turned her head slowly, her dark eyes wide with trepidation.

"Hey…hey, Glenda," she said unsteadily, hearing the guilt in her own voice.

Glenda's eyes narrowed, searching Emarie's face. "Kiddo, are you okay? I sent you home to rest and now you're here buying clothes?" she asked, glancing at the pile of clothes on the floor.

"Well…" Emarie started, searching her mind for an excuse. Any excuse.

"Well, what?"

"I'm feeling much better now after resting some and eating,"

Emarie offered, hoping Glenda would believe her.

"You sure about that? You looked as white as a ghost at the shop."

"Y-yes," Emaried stuttered, avoiding Glenda's penetrating gaze.

Glenda huffed and straightened to her full height, her hands on her hips. "Emarie Rose Gordon, what is going on? You're stuttering. We both know what that means!" She looked at the pile of clothes on the floor at Emarie's feet and pointed to them. "And that's another thing! When I came in to shoot the breeze with Jan, she mentioned that you were here looking for clothes for people in Ghana…something to do with your church. That sounds a little fishy to me. You've never mentioned anything about your church supporting an orphanage in Ghana. And why isn't your mom buying the clothes?" Glenda probed.

Emarie withered under the power of Glenda's interrogation. She could feel a fiery blush creep up her neck and onto her cheeks as she continued to evade Glenda's eyes.

Glenda pounced. "Ah ha! You're blushing! What gives? You've been acting weird ever since you fell asleep at the shop.

What's going on?"

Emarie's mind whirled as her heart beat wildly in her chest. "Nothing. Really! The orphanage is a new thing."

"It's a new thing?" Glenda repeated slowly, each word ringing with skepticism.

Emarie nodded without answering, staring at the floor.

"What's the name of the orphanage?" Glenda countered, watching Emarie closely.

"Ummm…"

"You don't know?" Glenda asked.

"No, it's just some orphanage," Emarie mumbled, feeling the blush rise to her forehead.

"You know I'm not buying this, right? I was young once…a long time ago," Glenda smirked. "I know a fib when I hear one. I was the master of the fib when I was your age. Like I said, you've been acting weird ever since you woke up at the work bench. I'm worried about you, Kiddo. It's time to fess up."

Emarie slowly looked up and stared into Glenda's troubled eyes. She knew how much Glenda loved her and that her concern was real. Next to her parents and grandparents, there was no one who loved her more than Glenda. She hated lying to her. She despised the dishonesty with all her heart. But how could she possibly tell Glenda about Victoria, Emmeline, Stefan and Lorna? How could she possibly believe that at this very moment Emarie had time travelers taking up residence in her treehouse? What rational person could believe such a thing? But Emarie also knew that Glenda had a wild imagination and a streak of eccentricity a mile wide. If anyone could believe in time travel, it would be Glenda. After all, Glenda's whole life had been a search for items from the past because of her love for the olden days. Maybe there was a reason Glenda had been the one to find the typewriter at the flea market in Millersburg. And maybe there was a reason the typewriter had ended up in Glenda's antique shop. Maybe Emarie was all wrong to be keeping the story from Glenda. Maybe it *was* time to tell her the truth. Emarie took a deep breath, exhaling the words that could forever change her relationship with Glenda. "Okay…well…I have these four friends…their names are Victoria, Emmeline, Stefan and Lorna…"

CHAPTER SIX

Their names caught and stuck in Emarie's throat as Glenda watched her with intense curiosity, waiting for the explanation about her four friends. Just when she'd absolutely resolved to tell Glenda the truth, she panicked. What if Glenda didn't believe her? What if Glenda thought she was crazy and went to her parents out of concern for her? What if they locked her up in a mental hospital along with the girls and Stefan? Then they might never make it back to 1902 to save Mr. Hill. Could she take the risk? At the last second, before the words crossed her lips, she decided she couldn't tell Glenda.

"Well?" Glenda prompted, impatiently waiting for an answer.

Emarie swallowed hard, holding Glenda's gaze with great difficulty. "They're kids I know from my home school co-op. Their dad…lost his job," Emarie said, nervously licking her dry lips.

"They're very proud and they don't want anyone to know what a struggle they're going through right now, but I wanted to help them with some clothes and some food…things like that…what little I can do," Emarie finished without stuttering once. She hated the thought that she might actually be getting good at lying.

Glenda stared at her, pondering what Emarie had just said. She pulled on one of her grey curls, deep in thought, all the while holding Emarie's gaze with her own. When Emarie looked away, the blush returning, Glenda slowly smiled. "I knew it! You're still fibbing. Well, Miss Emarie Rose, I don't know what you're up to, but I know you. I know you're one of the best people on this planet and that you wouldn't be up to anything wrong. But mark my words, I'll have my eye on you and I'm going to figure it out before all is said and done."

"But…" Emarie protested in alarm.

Glenda held up her finger. "Ah, no buts. I don't want you to keep lying and digging that hole of yours any deeper. I hope at some point you'll tell me what's going on, but until then, it gives me a chance to play detective," Glenda said enthusiastically, rubbing her hands together as she considered the juicy prospect.

Emarie did her best to throw Glenda off the scent. "Well, my friends are going to be at the Early American Days Festival tomorrow, so you can ask them yourselves!" Emarie insisted.

"Oh, is that right?"

"Yes! Honest to goodness!"

"Be careful how you use that word honest," Glenda responded. "Your reputation is everything. To be known as an honest person is worth a pot of gold. To be known as a dishonest person is to be the stench of the earth."

Emarie withered in shame, looking at the floor again, unable to meet Glenda's eyes.

"I thought so," Glenda responded, her voice softening. She bent down and kissed Emarie on the cheek. "I love you, Kiddo. I'll be here when you want to tell me what's going on. I'll see you at the festival tomorrow."

Emarie wrapped her arms around Glenda and hugged her tightly, tears pooling in her eyes. "See you tomorrow," she said softly.

After Glenda gave her one last squeeze before walking away, Emarie gathered up the pile of clothes and carried them to the counter where Jan greeted her with a smile, unaware of what had just transpired.

"Find everything you need for the orphanage?" Jan asked cheerfully.

"Yes…yeah," Emarie responded, shame burning in her chest.

"You okay? You seem upset."

"No, I'm okay. Just tired," Emarie answered, averting her eyes.

Jan nodded in acknowledgment and then proceeded to ring up and bag the clothes in record time. She waved enthusiastically as Emarie left the thrift store with two large bags, one in each hand.

As she walked into the Pizza Parlor to pick up the pizza just a few seconds later, Emarie suddenly realized that she didn't know how she was going to manage to get two big bags of clothes, a large pizza and four Coke's back to the treehouse on her own. She had to make a choice. She remembered how desperately hungry she'd been when she'd exited the portal into 1901. Stefan and the girls were probably starving by now. She had to choose whether to leave the clothes behind and take the food to them, or take the clothes, have them change quickly and then bring them back to the restaurant to eat. If she brought them to town tonight while Glenda was hot on her trail, she risked running into her and Glenda drilling them all with questions. It was a risk she couldn't take.

"Hey, Miss Tracy, could you watch these bags for me for just a little bit? I got some clothes at the thrift shop, but I can't carry them and the pizza and Coke's. I'll be back for them in a little bit, if that's okay."

"Sure, Honey, no problem! Just leave them on the floor there by the door."

Ten minutes later, Emarie stood at the base of the oak tree, breathing heavily from exertion. She'd walked as fast as she could, but it had been extremely awkward trying not to drop the pizza or the drinks while rushing. "Stefan! Stefan!" she called in a loud whisper. "I need your help to get this up there."

Stefan promptly opened the treehouse door and made his way down, skipping the last two steps as he jumped to the ground. "What is that?" he asked Emarie. "It smells delicious!"

"It's called pizza," Emarie answered, smiling. "It's a type of Italian food."

"Italy is near Albania. I'm sure it will be wonderful," Stefan responded, taking the box from her hands. "I'll carry it up." They struggled up the steps of the treehouse, but finally made it to the top and in – where they were promptly greeted by the famished time travelers.

"Thank goodness you're back!" Victoria exclaimed. "My stomach is starting to eat itself!"

"What is it?" Lorna questioned, eyeing the pizza box curiously.

Emarie set the Coke's down on the table beside the pizza box that Stefan had just laid there. "It's called pizza. It's a type of Italian food. It's a flat crust with tomato sauce, cheese and different toppings like meat, vegetables and even fruit sometimes." She lifted the lid and they all gathered around, eyeing it with great curiosity.

"Quite unusual," Emmeline commented as her mouth watered from inhaling the scent of the pizza.

Emarie grabbed paper towels from a cupboard and tore off individual pieces for each of them. She pulled slices of pizza from the box, laying them on the paper towels.

Lorna gasped. "You're touching the food with your hands! Why aren't you using a serving utensil?"

Emarie laughed. "Most people eat pizza with their hands."

"What?!" Victoria shrieked, aghast. "You want us to eat this with our hands?"

"Yes," Emarie giggled. "With your hands. Like this," she said, pulling a slice from the box and biting into it. The girls stepped back in shock, Victoria and Emmeline's gloved hands covering their mouths as they watched in fascinated horror.

"I'm willing to try anything at this point. I'm starving!" Stefan said, reaching for a piece of the pizza. He took a hefty bite, moaning blissfully as the flavors hit his taste buds. "Oh! Oh! It's delicious!"

After seeing Stefan's reaction, the girls tentatively stepped forward, each picking up a paper towel with a slice of pizza, hesitantly nibbling at the edges as if they were eating bugs rather than a tasty Italian staple. Within seconds their eyes widened in pleasure, and they began gobbling it down, reaching for piece after piece. After they drank the Coke to wash it down, Emarie laughed until her sides hurt as their deafening burps exploded like fireworks on the fourth of July.

CHAPTER SEVEN

Emarie walked close to the side of the buildings on Main Street with the others trailing closely behind her, trying to blend in with the people along the parade route. She held up the skirts of her Early American Days dress, enjoying the feel of the multiple layers she'd grown accustomed to wearing in 1901. She quickly glanced behind her to make sure Victoria, Emmeline, Lorna and Stefan hadn't lost track of her in the crowd. They were staring at everything in wide-eyed wonder, stunned by what they were seeing – the cars pulling in and out of the P&G IGA, the way the non-costumed people were dressed, and the music blaring from some of the floats in the parade. They looked stunned almost to the point of paralysis, but they inched forward slowly, keeping one eye trained on Emarie.

She led them toward the library little by little, saying hello and waving to most of the people along the parade route. She loved growing up in a small town and knowing almost everyone that lived there. It made her feel safe and loved.

Victoria, on Emarie's heels, leaned forward and whispered loudly in her ear. "Are you some kind of celebrity? Everyone knows you!"

Emarie smiled and shrugged. "Part of growing up in a small town, I guess. It's the best!"

Emmeline pushed forward to Emarie's side. "It reminds me of Main Street in Hornellsville…but newer…and with so many amazing and odd things! The motorized carriages…oh my goodness…fascinating!" Emmeline said, referring to the cars she'd seen. She sighed in delight, thoroughly enraptured with her surroundings.

"It probably reminds you of Hornellsville because it's a very old town. It kind of became a town in 1809, but it officially became incorporated as the town of Killbuck in 1874, so there are a lot of old buildings from that time that are still standing."

"1874 wasn't so long ago," Emmeline smiled.

Emarie laughed. "To you!"

Lorna joined them, ever eager to be a part of what was going on. "What are you talking about?" she asked, trying to chat with them and watch the parade at the same time.

"Just about the town…how old it is," Emarie answered. She stopped at the corner before rounding on to Front Street. The four of them stopped in their tracks, waiting for her signal. Emarie looked around, scanning the crowd and the sidewalks for Glenda. She didn't see her anywhere. "Okay, come on…the library is just a few doors up."

They walked in a single file line past the Snowside Coffee Shop and the dentist's office before finally making it to the library. Emarie pulled on the door, praying for it to be unlocked. To her relief, it was open. She hurriedly waved them in. For several moments, they all stood silently in the small library, looking around and orienting themselves.

Lorna broke the silence, pointing to the computers along the back wall. "Are those the com…pu…ters?" she asked slowly, trying to remember the word.

"Yes," Emarie responded, moving toward the desks. "Come on…let's see what we can find out!" Emarie sat down in one of the chairs in front of a computer while the others gathered around,

barely able to breathe as they waited to see what the modern marvel

would be able to tell them about Brandon Hill's fate.

They all gasped when the computer booted up and words

flashed across the screen.

"What in the world?" Stefan breathed, barely able to make sense of

what he was seeing.

Lorna screamed, biting her tongue in the process. "Ahh!"

she groaned in pain.

Victoria rolled her eyes at Lorna then moved closer to the

monitor, studying the words and images flashing across the screen.

"How? How is it able to do this?"

"It would take me explaining over a hundred years of science

to you for it to make sense…and I'm not that good at science,"

Emarie joked.

"It's so odd. Like a typewriter…you hit them, and they make

words," she said, pointing to the keyboard and then the monitor.

"But the keys are flat and not connected to anything. I can't grasp it

at all," Emmeline said, her voice hushed with awe.

"Okay, here we go," Emarie said, her heart pounding in her

chest as she typed the words: *Brandon Hill Guard Attack New York City 1902* into the Google search bar. Instantly, a myriad of links popped up.

"Oh! What does it mean? It's all about Father!" Emmeline cried.

"When I click on these sentences, it will tell us about your father and the attack on the guard and what happened," Emarie responded, looking over her shoulder at them. "Are you sure you want to know?" she asked uneasily.

"We don't have a choice. We need to know," Victoria said, squaring her shoulders as tears stung her eyes.

"Okay." Emarie took a deep breath and clicked on the first link. A Wikipedia entry opened up, revealing the story of Brandon Hill's fate. They all read the words hungrily, poring over the first few sentences as if their very lives depended on it.

Victoria's hand flew to her mouth, gasping, tears falling onto her cheeks. Emmeline began to sob, and turned to her sister, embracing her.

"Thank God!" Stefan finally breathed. "He didn't hang. Innocent! And the guard survived!"

Lorna clapped and jumped up and down while Emarie laughed joyfully through a veil of grateful tears. "We need to keep reading. We need to find out exactly what happened. The typewriter sent you here for a reason. There may be some information you need to take back to 1902 in order to save your father," she said to Victoria and Emmeline.

"But the article said he was innocent of the crime," Stefan protested.

"But he may have only been found innocent because of information you take back to 1902," Emarie responded.

"Time travel…it makes my head hurt!" Emmeline wailed.

The five of them turned back to the monitor and continued to read for several minutes before Emarie declared loudly, quoting the Wikipedia article. "Here! Brandon Hill was exonerated by anonymous information given to the police!"

"But it doesn't say what the information was or why the person who gave it to the police had to remain anonymous," Emmeline said in a rush of excitement as she continued to read over Emarie's shoulder.

"Let's try another article," Emarie responded excitedly,

hitting the back arrow. She clicked on several more articles, but nothing they read revealed who had provided the information that had cleared Brandon Hill of such a heinous crime.

"I don't understand," Victoria said. "Why isn't there more information available in these…writings…about what happened? About how my father's name was cleared and who *actually* committed the crime. My father is a wealthy, well-known man. The details would be of great interest to the general public."

"There has to be a reason," Stefan responded, deep in thought.

"We have to get back to 1902 to work this out!" Victoria said, her words filled with urgency. They all nodded, feeling the weight of responsibility resting heavily on their shoulders.

As they pondered what would come next, someone behind them cleared their throat. Emarie froze, recognizing the familiar sound. "Emarie, *what* is going on here?" Glenda asked very softly, her eyes trained like lasers on the five young people before her.

They turned as one, silent for several moments before Emarie finally asked, her voice quivering, "How long have you been standing there?"

"Long enough," Glenda replied solemnly. "Long enough."

CHAPTER EIGHT

Emarie cleared her throat, searching for the right words, but none would come. It was as if her vocal chords were completely paralyzed. The others stared at Glenda, terrified.

"I'm waiting," Glenda said, moving several steps closer to the group of frightened young people.

"You'll never believe it," Emarie finally managed to say weakly, her voice croaking like a frog. "My mom and dad love me more than anyone in the world and they wouldn't even believe me!"

"Try me," Glenda responded, eyeing Victoria and Emmeline's beautiful dresses, then Lorna and Stefan's servants' garb.

"I don't know how anyone could possibly believe it. It can't be! It's not possible…yet it is!"

"I'm *waiting*," Glenda said, her tone very clearly indicating that she wanted an explanation – and *now*.

Emarie sighed, then plunged in, realizing there was no way to evade Glenda any longer. "Do you remember how I said the typewriter keys were buzzing when I touched the Underwood No. 5 in your shop yesterday?"

"Yes."

"That I felt the buzzing, but you didn't?" Emarie added.

"Yes," Glenda responded, listening carefully.

"When you went to shelve things, I put a piece of paper in the typewriter and began typing. After I typed words onto the paper, this weird and powerful whirlwind swept through the room and clouds formed…and I saw images in the clouds…"

"Images?" Glenda interrupted.

"Like a vision. Images of a white horse drawing a carriage, a train, children crying, a sad man at a well pump…"

"Go on," Glenda prompted.

Emarie licked her lips and swallowed hard. "After that, the whirlwind lifted me out of the swivel chair and the next thing I knew, I was in the air above the shop looking down on it. I screamed for you and tried to free myself, but I couldn't. Then, somehow…I don't know how…I fell asleep…and while I was asleep, the whirlwind carried me back in time…to 1901." Emarie paused, searching Glenda's face for signs of disbelief or doubt. The lined and wrinkled face stared back at her, searching her own face for signs of deceit.

"Keep going," Glenda urged, her eyes fixed on Emarie.

"It was the typewriter…the typewriter opened a time traveling portal! The typewriter took me there and the typewriter brought me back…and yesterday, the typewriter brought my friends from 1901 here to me. Hill!" Emarie abruptly yelled, causing Glenda to take a step backward. "Remember? Remember how I went crazy when you noticed the engraved plate on the side of the typewriter that said, *Property of the Hill Wallpaper Co.*? Their father," she said, pointing to Victoria and Emmeline, "is Brandon Hill. He owns the Hill Wallpaper Company. And he's in trouble! He's been falsely accused of attacking a man and we believe that's why my friends were sent to my…I mean, to *our* time…to get information from here in the future that will help save him in the past!"

Glenda loudly exhaled the breath she'd been holding and

pressed the palms of her hands to her throbbing temples. "Time travel?" she questioned, her expression skeptical.

"Yes!" Victoria said, stepping forward. "We didn't believe it, either, when Emarie appeared in our time! But she was able to tell us that President McKinley was going to be shot the day before it actually happened. We knew then that she was telling the truth! And we watched the typewriter carry her back here to 2018...we witnessed the portal opening with our own eyes!"

"We wouldn't lie to you," Emmeline added, clasping her hands together as if she were praying. "Emarie told us so much about you when she was with us in 1901. We know how much she loves you. We would never deceive someone so important to Emarie!" Stefan and Lorna nodded silently, affirming Emmeline's statement.

Glenda stared at them, at a complete loss for words. Questions, confusion, thoughts, ideas, doubts, disbelief, all bounced through her mind like a wind-tossed tumbleweed.

Lorna slowly walked up to Glenda and gently took the older woman's hand while looking up at her, her dark eyes shining with sincerity. "Please believe us. Please trust Emarie."

Glenda squeezed the small girl's hand warmly, utterly gob smacked. "I don't know what to believe. This is beyond fantastical!"

"I know it is," Emaried responded, rising from the chair in front of the computer monitor. "It took time for me to accept that it was real and not a dream. And even when I was transported back and woke up at the work bench, I thought it still might be a dream…until you pointed out the plate with the Hill Wallpaper Company name on it. Then I knew…it had all been real!"

Glenda again considered each of them, trying to come to a conclusion. A thought suddenly occurred to her. "The Rapid-Fire Liar Test!" she exclaimed.

"The…*what*?" Emarie asked, confused.

"The Rapid-Fire Liar Test," Glenda repeated. "A person asks a series of rapid-fire questions and if the person who's being questioned hesitates or has to search their mind for an answer that would come quickly to a person who's telling the truth, then you know they're lying! When a person is telling the truth, the truth comes naturally to them and they can answer quickly without hesitation. The Rapid-Fire Liar Test!"

Emarie laughed. "Ooooookay. Only you would come up with something like that!"

Glenda walked toward the group, stopping just in front of them. "Okay, are you ready?" she asked Victoria, Emmeline, Lorna and Stefan. They all nodded silently, bracing themselves. "I'm going to ask questions that you all should be able to easily and quickly answer," she instructed. "Got it?" They all nodded silently again, indicating that they were ready. "Who is the president?" Glenda asked, firing the first volley.

"Theodore Roosevelt," they all answered immediately.

"Who is the Vice-President?" Glenda countered quickly.

"Charles Fairbanks!"

"What is your mother's name?" Glenda asked, pointing to Victoria and Emmeline.

"Eva!" Victoria and Emmeline instantly answered.

"What is your address?"

"424 Ivy Lane, Hornellsville, New York!" the four answered as one voice.

"Do you have a family pet?"

"Yes!"

"A cat or dog?"

"Dog!" they answered in unison.

"What year were you born?" she asked, pointing to Lorna.

"1891!"

"And what year were you born?" Glenda asked Stefan, without pausing.

"1884, Ma'am!"

"And you?" Glenda demanded, pointing to Emmeline.

"1886!"

"And you?" she asked, finally pointing to Victoria.

"1884!" Victoria responded triumphantly.

Glenda paused to catch her breath, watching the four strangers carefully, mulling and considering. At last, an enormous smile spread across her face and her eyes gleamed with the glorious thrill of a new-found adventure. "Well, my friends, we have a lot to talk about! I want the whole story from beginning to end. Tell me everything that happened while Emarie was with you in 1901…absolutely *everything*!"

CHAPTER NINE

Glenda held up her hand to hold them off. "But wait…not here. Someone could overhear us, and they'd think the whole lot of us are crazy! I'm going to take you to my cabin. You can tell me all about it there." She took on the demeanor of a spy on a top-secret mission as she signaled to them to follow her.

"But Glenda, your cabin is a couple miles away," Emarie protested. "Isn't there somewhere else we could talk?"

Glenda shook her head as she conspiratorially looked through the window of the library door. "We can't take a chance that someone would overhear us. It's the best place to talk. We'll be there in no time!"

"You're used to walking from there to your shop and back every day. It'll be no time for you, but it will seem like forever to us…especially in these shoes," she retorted, lifting the hem of her long dress, exposing her old-fashioned dress boots.

"I never took you for a lazy bones, Emarie," Glenda countered. "Let's do this! It's by far the safest place to talk." Victoria and the others stood silently, watching the back and forth between Emarie and Glenda.

"But my mom and dad…"

"Oh, come on, Emarie, you run these streets all day long and only make it home just before dark most days. They won't wonder where you are for hours."

Emarie shrugged her shoulders in defeat and then nodded to the others, giving the go-ahead. They left the library in a single file line, trailing behind Glenda like a gaggle of goslings following their mother.

She led them out of the library and turned right onto Water Street at the end of the sidewalk. The parade-goers paid no attention to the group passing by as they intently watched a procession of marching bands followed by the local Girl Scout troop and then proud military veterans waving to the grateful crowd. Glenda forged ahead at a fast clip, leading them down Water Street until they were out of the downtown area and walking along Killbuck Creek. After walking for a long while, they came into the wooded and swampy area of Shreve Swamp, the sound of birds chirping and frogs croaking welcoming them. A multitude of plant life burst from beneath the water to the surface, decorating the swamp with vibrant greenery. Both living and dead trees dotted the expanse, their roots submerged beneath the murky water. Fallen branches and small sticks floated randomly on the serene surface, meandering to nowhere in particular.

"I've never seen anything quite like it," Stefan said admiringly.

Glenda looked over her shoulder, smiling. "It's a lonely area, but it's beautiful," she commented. "That's why I chose to live here. It suits me perfectly." And with those words, she stopped short. "And there it is," she said with pride, pointing to a ramshackle cabin on the edge of the swamp's waters. A timeworn rocking chair sat on the front porch, swaying slightly back and forth in the gentle wind that had suddenly begun blowing. An old metal horse trough in the weed-dotted front yard was filled with colorful summer flowers beginning to wilt as fall loomed.

Victoria coughed slightly in an effort to suppress her

reaction. "It's a most…unusual…home," she said politely.
Emmeline elbowed Victoria, glaring at her.

Glenda laughed good-naturedly. "Oh, it's okay, you don't
need to be polite about it. I know it's not in the best shape anymore,
but I love it. It's all mine and it's comfortable. It may not be
everyone's cup of tea, but it's my cup of tea," she beamed. She led
them up the rickety front steps and through the front door scarred by
a large crack down the middle of the wood.

Lorna gasped and everyone except Emarie felt the same
emotion – complete surprise. The ramshackle and unkempt exterior
had opened up into a warm, cozy and inviting interior. Every
surface and wall were an ode to Glenda's eccentricity, but somehow
it all came together in a way that made a person feel as if they were
at home and at peace.

Emmeline smiled broadly, gently touching Glenda's arm in
acknowledgment. "It's simply lovely."

"Aw, thanks," Glenda responded, genuinely moved by
Emmeline's kind words. "Now, come on, let's sit down," she said,
abruptly shifting gears. "I'm ready to hear this whole tale!" she
grinned, rubbing her hands together in excitement.

They all found places to sit on the comfortable tweed couch and the worn but cozy chairs surrounding it. Glenda took a seat in her beloved Lazyboy, her eyes wide with expectation.

Emarie began the story, continuing from where she'd left off with finding herself suddenly transported to a strange place and wondering if she was in some kind of Victorian reality show after she saw the people dancing in the Hills' ballroom. Lorna picked up the thread, telling Glenda how she'd found Emarie in the kitchen and then run off in terror when Emarie told her she was a time traveler. Glenda laughed heartily when Lorna said she wondered if Emarie had escaped from a lunatic asylum.

Stefan then explained how he'd found Emarie in the stables after she'd run away from the house – and how he'd been flabbergasted to find her so scantily clad.

Victoria jumped in next, relaying how she'd confronted Emarie in the stables after Lorna had come to her with the story about Emarie claiming to be a time traveler.

Emmeline finally spoke, explaining her introduction to Emarie and how she and Victoria had waited with dread to see if Emarie's prediction about President McKinley would come to pass.

From there, every detail of Emarie's time in the past was explained to Glenda in minute detail – from clothing Emarie to the attack by the robbers while riding to town in the carriage, to the failed attempt to open the time portal with the Underwood No. 3 in the post office, to rescuing Robert and the tale of Gabardine Fusk, to the thievery and deception of Conrad Beesly and Senora Sierra tracking him down with her axe, to their time in jail, to returning Robert to his family, to Emarie leaving 1901 in the whirlwind and clouds – and finally to the story of Mr. Hill being falsely accused of attacking a man now in a coma and their belief that the Underwood No. 5 had sent them to 2018 for Emarie's help.

When the tale had finally came to an end after the space of several hours, Glenda exhaled a giant breath, dumbfounded by the account of events that each of the children had provided. She sat in silence for several minutes, just staring at them, considering the implications of all she'd been told. She had always fantasized about the idea of time travel, but to know that it was actually possible – and that five people who had traveled through time were sitting here right in front of her – made her mind reel in wonder and confusion.

"Are you okay?" Emarie finally ventured, asking the

question they were all thinking.

"I think I am," Glenda said, holding a hand to her head as if doing so would calm the storm of perplexing thoughts. "It's just an incredible story. Absolutely incredible!"

As if to put an exclamation point on her bewilderment, an enormous boom of thunder suddenly sounded, causing them all to gasp and jump. In the next seconds, a downpour of rain began battering the roof of the dilapidated cabin, and Emarie groaned in disbelief.

She ran to the front door and yanked it open, staring into the eerie greyness that had descended on the swamp in the deluge of rain. "Oh, no!" she wailed. "There's no way we're going to make it back before dark in this mess! My parents are going to freak out!"

CHAPTER TEN

Glenda rushed to Emarie's side, peering out at the suddenly dark sky. "Oh, dear," she muttered.

"What are we going to do?" Emarie cried, turning to Glenda. "You don't have a car or a cell phone! My parents are going to kill me!"

"Kill you?!" Lorna shrieked, aghast.

"Oh, no…not for real!" Emarie reassured as she turned to face Lorna. "It's just an expression…a figure of speech…they would never kill me!"

"Thank goodness!" Lorna breathed, greatly relieved.

Stefan came up beside Glenda and Emarie, gazing out at the storm raging across the swamp. "It looks perilous. What should we do?" he asked. Emmeline screamed as a bolt of lightning flashed across the sky and hit nearby. They instinctively took several steps backward, their ears ringing from the power of the strike.

Glenda shook her head. "I don't see how we could possibly risk going out into it. Let's close the door. It's not safe to be standing in the doorway with this lightning." She shut the door tightly and Emarie and Stefan turned with her to join the others. Glenda hugged Emarie tightly, sensing how distraught she was. "It's going to be okay. We'll figure it out."

"I don't see how. You don't have a landline or a cell phone," Emarie said despairingly.

"What's a landline…and a cell phone…is that like the telephone Mr. Bell invented?" Victoria asked, intensely curious.

"Yes!" Glenda answered enthusiastically. "A cell phone is a small, wireless telephone that you can carry with you anywhere…in your pocket…in your hand. A landline is what we call telephones now that aren't cell phones…they're attached by a line to the house…much like the telephones in your time."

"Father has resisted having telephones installed in our homes," Emmeline interjected. "But he does have several in the company offices. I'm not sure why he has such a strong objection to having a telephone…"

"I imagine it's for the sake of peace," Victoria said ruefully. "He most likely does not want to be bothered after a long day of work."

Emmeline nodded. "You're probably right."

"What are we going to do?" Emarie groaned, cutting off the conversation about the telephone. "I don't want them to worry. I know they'll be worried sick!"

Glenda grimaced. "Honey, we don't have a choice. We can't risk going out. I'm sorry…it's my fault…I insisted on coming here to talk."

Emmeline stepped forward and took Emarie's hand. "Why don't we play a game? Something to get our mind off the storm. And then we'll head back just as soon as the weather breaks."

Glenda jumped at Emmeline's suggestion. "Yes! Let's do that! Let's play a game to get our minds off it like Emmeline suggested. What game from our time would you like to introduce them to?" she asked Emarie, winking.

Emarie considered the question as she came to terms with the fact that there was nothing left to do but ride out the storm. "How about Clue? That's a fun one. I think they'll be up for solving a mystery," she smiled.

"Oh, I love mysteries!" Emmeline affirmed. "Have you read the Sherlock Holmes mystery, *The Hound of the Baskervilles*?" she asked excitedly.

"Yes! That's an amazing story!" Glenda responded.

"It was released in America earlier this year in our time and I was halfway through it when the typewriter brought us here."

"Well, then, I won't give away the ending," Glenda laughed.

"How do you play Clue?" Stefan interrupted.

"Each of us will be different characters in the game...and we'll be given clues about the events of a murder...and the first one to solve the mystery wins the game!"

"That sounds so fun!" Lorna said, clapping.

"I've never heard of any type of game where you solve a murder, but it does sound quite thrilling," Emmeline added enthusiastically.

"Wait! Why don't we tell scary stories!" Victoria exclaimed, her eyes gleaming. "A storm is the perfect time to tell scary stories!"

"That's an excellent idea, too!" Glenda agreed. "How about we do that?" she asked them. After they had all nodded in complete agreement to the new idea, Glenda said, "Great! Let's grab a snack and then I'll start a fire. I've got a story for you that's been part of our town lore for generations. It's the bomb!"

"A bomb?" Lorna nearly screamed.

"Not a real bomb," Glenda assured her, laughing. "It's just a phrase that means something is really exciting!"

Twenty minutes later, after Lorna's fears about "the bomb" had been calmed and they'd had their snacks, they sat down in a half circle on the floor in front of the fireplace, the storm furiously crashing and pounding outside. Lorna shivered in fear, clinging to Emarie as she waited for the story to begin.

Glenda sat directly in front of the crackling fire, her expression transformed into one who has been carried away to another place and time. "Long, long ago," she began in a hushed whisper, "there were two children – a brother and a sister – who lived on the edge of this swamp much like I do now. They had lost both of their parents to small pox the year before and they lived alone in their one room cabin, struggling every day to survive on their own with no one to help them. The swamp was wild then...a place of danger. One night, the brother and sister were out on the waters of the swamp, desperately lost in a storm after a full day of fishing. The pelting rain blinded them, causing them to turn in circles. Confusion and terror held them in its vice-like grip. Then suddenly, out of nowhere, they saw a covering where they could escape the storm…a tangle of broken tree limbs, branches and leaves that had snaked and wound together naturally to form something like a small room. They rowed their small boat to the covering, relieved. As they sat in the enclosure, soaked to the bone and their teeth chattering, they suddenly heard a sound that sent the chill in their bones directly to the center of their sou. A low moaning…a low moaning that pierced the blackness of the night. They grabbed on to each other and held on with all their strength. As the sound grew closer, the sister sat up straight and leaned forward, listening as if her very life depended on it. 'Wait! I think it's mother…it sounds like mother…moaning the way she did when she was so sick! Has she come back to us?' the young girl asked her brother, her eyes wide with shock and uncertainty. The brother swallowed hard, listening with all of his might. He finally nodded to his sister. 'Yes! I think you're right…I think it *is* Mother! We need to go to her!' he whispered urgently. Together, they rowed the boat out of the covering, venturing ever so slowly out of the enclosure and into the storm-ravaged night, following the sound. Just when they were upon it, they froze, their hearts consumed with horror as a hideous monster slowly rose up out of the swamps' waters, looming over them. It extended its long, leafy arms toward them and opened its slimy jaws, its razor-sharp teeth bared in hunger…"

And just then, as Glenda came to the terrifying climax of the story, the front door of the cabin cracked and splintered from top to bottom as something on the other side pounded the door with savage strength, causing them all to erupt in screams of wild terror.

CHAPTER ELEVEN

"It's the swamp monster!" Lorna screamed. She scrambled to her feet and dove over the top of the couch, rolling over the back and onto the floor, trembling from head to toe as she crouched in fear.

Victoria, Emmeline and Emarie clung to one another, terrified out of their minds. "What is it?!" Emmeline shrieked.

Stefan and Glenda rose to their feet, their hearts pounding. "Let me see…let me see! It's not a swamp monster, that's for darn sure! Just hold on," she calmed, "I'll see who it is."

"I'm coming with you," Stefan said protectively, following Glenda to the door.

Glenda took a deep breath before pulling the door open. As she did, the force of the wind gust blew it out of her hand and it nearly smacked her in the face as she quickly side-stepped the impact of the damaged door. Brian and Marci Gordon stood on the doorstep, drenched from head to toe. Glenda breathed a huge sigh of relief. "Hurry! Come in!" she urged, trying to close the ruined door behind them as they stepped into the room.

"Is Emarie here?" Marci asked pleadingly. "She didn't come home and some people at the parade said they saw her with you!" At that moment, she spotted Emarie in front of the fireplace and she screamed in relief, running to her daughter and pulling her up from the floor into a tight hug. "Thank God!" she cried.

Lorna slowly stood up, peeking over the back of the couch. Stefan, Victoria and Emmeline froze, holding their breath as they waited for the unknown that was to come.

"I'm so sorry! It's my fault," Glenda rushed to explain. "I kind of insisted on showing Emarie's…ah…new…friends…uh…that she met at the festival…ah…my little slice of heaven here on the swamp. We didn't expect it to rain and once it started, it was too dangerous to go out into it. And you know…crazy Glenda doesn't have a car or cell phone," she said, laughing awkwardly.

"It's okay," Brian Gordon said, buying Glenda's story.

"All's well that ends well, but we may have to come up with a check-in policy from here on out now that we've had the scare of our lives." He walked up to Marci and Emarie and wrapped himself around them, forming a group hug. After a few seconds they drew apart and Brian looked around the room at Lorna standing behind the couch, then Victoria and Emmeline still sitting on the floor by the fireplace, and Stefan near the front door. "Can you introduce us to your new friends?" he said to Emarie, smiling.

"Umm…uh…sure!" Emarie said, trying desperately to act normal and form a cover story all at the same time. "Stefan," she said, pointing to him, "Victoria and Emmeline," she added, sweeping her hand toward them, "and Lorna," she said, pointing to the frightened young scullery maid behind the couch.

"Nice to meet you all," Brian responded welcomingly.

"Glenda said that you're friends of Emarie's from the festival…where are you all from?" Marci asked in a friendly manner, making conversation.

Stefan, Victoria, Emmeline and Lorna looked at one another frantically, their eyes wide with panic. After several seconds, Stefan broke the silence, speaking for the four of them. "We came over from…" he said, his eyes darting to Emarie.

"Millersburg!" Emarie rushed to interject.

"Yes, from Millersburg. We came over from Millersburg for the Early American Days Festival. We were talking to Emarie about Killbuck…she was telling us about some of the history of the town…and then she introduced us to Glenda," he concluded, the palms of his hands sweating as he waited for a reaction.

"Oh, nice!" Marci replied, her normally suspicious nature not on high-alert with the relief of finding Emarie safe. "Emarie's kind of an amateur historian about Killbuck. She loves her hometown!"

"Well, let's get you home," Brian Gordon said to Emarie, patting her head. "How are you all getting home?" he asked, assuming they were brothers and sisters.

"Umm…Stefan drove…he has his license," Emarie said, wishing she could bite off her own tongue for lying so much.

"I didn't see a car out front," Brian responded, pointing toward the front door.

"I…I left it in town…we walked here. It was such a nice day," Stefan said, coughing to clear his tight throat.

"Well, we can drop you off in town," Brian offered.

"I think we're going to stay a little longer," Victoria said hurriedly, standing up and walking toward Brian and Marci. "We were having fun telling scary stories and talking, so we'll just hang out here until the storm clears and then we'll walk back to the car…"

"But it's dark now. I don't know if that's a good idea," Marci said, her expression betraying her concern.

"Oh, we'll be fine," Victoria assured her. "We're from the country…we're used to this…and we'll have Stefan with us," she smiled.

"I don't know," Brian countered, looking skeptical. "It's really bad out. I'm not sure this storm is clearing up tonight. It really would be best if we drop you off. Where are you parked?"

Stefan shifted uncomfortably, not sure what to do or say. He very subtly looked at Emarie for help, but Emarie shrugged her shoulders, at a complete loss against her dad's faultless logic. "Well…we…we parked…"

"At the P&G IGA," Emmeline chimed in, recalling the name of the grocery store.

"Oh, perfect…that's right on our way home," Brian said. "Glenda, back me up here. Don't you think it's best for us to drop the kids off? This storm isn't going anywhere tonight."

Glenda nervously licked her lips. "Well…I guess so…probably," she said, feeling cornered since it was obviously the best thing to do under normal circumstances.

"Do you have a cell phone?" Marci asked. "Maybe you should let your parents know you're okay…if you haven't already."

"No, we don't have a cell phone," Victoria responded. "But I'm sure they know we're okay. They always feel good about us being out and about as long as Stefan is with us," she smiled brightly.

"Okay, well, let's go," Brian said. "It sounds like we're getting a slight break in the storm, but it may not last long. You kids should head for home as soon as possible." With that, he headed toward the front door and stopped, examining the split down the middle. "Yikes! Sorry about this Glenda. I can come back tomorrow to fix it."

"Don't worry about it," Glenda responded. "It already had a crack in it to begin with. It's not your fault. I can handle it."

"Okay…but let me know if you have any problems with it. I'm happy to help clean up a mess I created," he grimaced. "Okay, kids, let's head out," he called.

As he turned toward the door, he didn't catch the frightened and alarmed looks exchanged between his daughter and the four young people who had traveled from a much further distance than Millersburg, Ohio.

CHAPTER TWELVE

Emarie, Stefan and Victoria sat cramped in the back of Emarie's parents' mini-van, Stefan and Victoria holding on for dear life as they traveled at unimaginable speeds in the Gordon's "horseless carriage." Emmeline and Lorna sat rigidly upright in the captain's seats, barely breathing.

"What are we going to do after they leave us at the grocery?" Victoria whispered frantically.

Emarie wracked her brain, trying to come up with a plan. Finally, she said, "Just go inside the store to make it look good…then after we pull away, walk back to the treehouse."

"But it's pouring down rain!" Victoria objected.

"I don't know what else to do. You can change into the clothes I got you once you get back to the treehouse…and you have warm blankets now," Emarie said, referring to the blankets and pillows she'd secreted to the treehouse earlier that day.

"I'm not certain I remember the way back," Stefan whispered uncertainly.

"Take Front Street out of town and turn right onto the first lane and follow it to our house. You'll recognize it, and you know the way to the treehouse from there," Emarie explained hurriedly.

Just as she finished giving Stefan directions, Brian Gordon pulled into the parking lot of the P&G IGA. "Which one's yours?" he asked, looking at Stefan in the rearview mirror. Stefan scanned the parking lot and randomly pointed to a vehicle in the far corner. Brian nodded. "I'll drop you off by your car so you don't get soaked," he said, turning the wheel of the minivan and heading in the direction of the blue Ford Focus Stefan had pointed out.

"No!" Victoria bellowed, causing Emarie's dad to look back in alarm.

"What?" he asked, disconcerted by her loud objection.

"We would…we would…like to go into the store," she said rapidly, an embarrassed blush flushing her cheeks.

"Oh, okay, sure," Brian laughed awkwardly.

"I apologize for my tone," Victoria said politely, her turn of the century manners on full display.

"No worries!" Brian responded good-naturedly.

"What does he mean by 'no worries'?" Victoria whispered to Emarie.

"It means you don't have to worry that he was offended by your tone," Emarie explained. Victoria nodded, feeling accomplished as she gained knowledge about this strange new world.

Brian pulled up to the front entrance of the store and pushed the button that remotely opened each of the side doors of the minivan. Lorna gasped and pointed, and Emmeline's eyes widened in fear and disbelief. Both girls were convinced that a ghost had suddenly inhabited the Gordon's automobile.

Marci Gordon chuckled as she looked back at the two young ladies in the captain's seats. "Haven't you girls ever seen remote doors?"

"Remote doors? No...no," Emmeline responded shakily, finding it difficult to drag her eyes from the magical door.

"It's really not a big deal," Marci said. "It's a new minivan, so it has all the bells and whistles."

"Bells and whistles? Where are they?" Lorna asked. Brian and Marci laughed, amused by the quirkiness of Emarie's new friends.

"Alright, let's take our leave," Victoria directed, before any more damage could be done. They stood up and slowly filed out of the van, waving to Emarie and her parents as the minivan pulled away, Emarie's worried face watching them from the rear window as a crash of thunder suddenly sounded.

"There's no way we can walk back to the treehouse in this thunder and lightning," Stefan said. "We need to go inside the grocery until this storm slows some."

Resigned to the situation, they turned toward the entrance, eager to see the inside of a modern grocery store. They looked at the two glass doors with no doorknobs, completely confused. "How do we open it?" Emmeline asked. They stepped forward, examining the glass carefully. Stefan ran his hands along the seam in the middle, tugging at it to no avail.

"This is supposed to be a time of modern marvels and they don't even have knobs on their doors!" Victoria complained, disgusted.

"They might be magic doors like the automobile had!" Lorna suggested excitedly.

"Oh, that's true," Victoria agreed, staring at the door, perplexed. "Then why isn't it opening?"

"That's why it's not opening," Stefan said, pointing to a sign on the glass door, reading it out loud. "Closing early for Early American Days." They groaned in unison, utterly discouraged as they faced the prospect of walking back to the treehouse in the raging storm.

"There has to be somewhere that's open for business," Stefan said, turning back toward Front Street, gazing into the murky darkness dimly lit by streetlights.

"It appears that everything is closed at the moment – and the festival has shut down. It must be because this storm is so horrible," Victoria lamented.

"Look! A museum!" Emmeline said, pointing to a storefront sign that read: Killbuck Valley Museum. "I can see just a bit of light coming from inside. Let's try there!" she said excitedly, always eager to explore a new museum. They dashed across the street as the driving rain pelted fiercely, soaking them from head to toe as the girls' long skirts whipped in the savage wind. Stefan pulled on the door handle and thanked the good Lord when it opened. They rushed in and stood just inside the doorway, rainwater running off them and puddling on the floor.

"I don't think anyone is here," Victoria said quietly, as the absolute stillness and near darkness of the museum set in.

"Oh, my!" Emmeline exclaimed, pointing.

Their eyes were immediately drawn to the right of the room, startled and joyfully surprised by what they saw. "It's from our time!" Lorna shouted, running over to the display of a turn of the century schoolroom. She ran her hands over the antique wrought iron and wood school desks and the books sitting upon them, then walked over to the wood burning stove in the far corner where a life size cut out of a teacher stood between it and a large blackboard. The girls joined her, weaving in and out of the school desks, amazed by the display.

"They must truly have an appreciation for our time to have such an exhibit," Emmeline said pensively, feeling suddenly homesick.

"Come and see this!" Stefan called, popping his head from

around the corner of the next room. The girls hurried after him, stopping short in an adjoining room as they gazed at a multitude of glass cases filled with fossils of plants, animals, seashells and even mastodon tusks.

"This is absolutely amazing!" Victoria exclaimed, moving from case to case, reading the display cards explaining the origin of each fossil. Emmeline and Stefan trailed behind her, completely absorbed as they peered closely at every specimen. Lorna, bored with them reading every card, wandered into the next room. Several minutes later, they halted in their steps as her ear-splitting scream shattered their concentration. They ran to her, stopping short in horror as they were surrounded by hundreds of wild animals, their teeth bared and ready to attack.

CHAPTER THIRTEEN

Stefan stepped forward and cupped his hand over Lorna's mouth, stifling her scream. "Lorna, they're not real! They're stuffed!"

The scream died in Lorna's throat as her eyes adjusted to the darkness and she realized that Stefan was right.

"I thought they were real, too!" Emmeline gasped, her heart still pounding like thunder.

"I have to admit, I believed they were alive as well," Victoria added, feeling foolish. She tentatively began walking around the room, entranced by the hundreds of animals that had been preserved by various taxidermists. Emmeline, Stefan and Lorna followed her, Lorna holding on to the back of Emmeline's dress for comfort. A moose, owls, bobcats, squirrels, a gazelle, badgers, large birds of prey of every shape and size, a black bear – it was an amazing menagerie of local wildlife that had been faithfully preserved for the public to appreciate and enjoy.

"We need to get out of here!" Lorna insisted as she turned and tugged at Stefan's shirtsleeve, still terrified of the animals that stared at her with unmoving, glass eyes.

"I think that's probably a good idea," Stefan said, calling the girls to follow him back to the front room of the museum.

"Please remove me from this den of horrors!" Lorna wailed as they stood near the front door near the old-fashioned school display.

"That's a bit melodramatic, wouldn't you say?" Victoria snickered. "The animals were fascinating."

"Nonetheless," Emmeline countered, realizing that Lorna was about to break out in hysterics, "let's find another place to wait out the storm."

"Well, where?" Victoria pressed. "It doesn't seem that any place is open for business."

Emmeline peered into the night through the glass of the museum's front door. "Look!" She pointed at an older building across the street, diagonal to the museum. "There are a few people going into that building across the street. It has a large green D over the doors…lit up somehow…and a type of glass booth in the front. I wonder what it could be?" The others crowded around her at the front door, looking out.

"It resembles the ticket booths for the theaters back home," Victoria mused.

"Oh, could it be a theater?" Lorna asked dreamily. "How wonderful!"

"Well, let's try it," Stefan said resolutely. With that, the girls gathered up the skirts of their dresses and they slowly opened the door and stepped out, huddling together under the museum's porch roof, dreading the thought of stepping into the driving rain again. "It's now or never!" Stefan urged, taking Lorna's hand as he plunged into the downpour. Victoria and Emmeline followed, and within thirty seconds they had run past the empty ticket booth and into the building, gazing around in curiosity.

"What…is…*that*?" Lorna whispered, pointing a trembling finger toward an enormous cutout of a dinosaur whose mouth was open wide, exposing menacing, razor-sharp teeth.

"It looks very much like a rendering of the fossilized bones of the Dynamosaurus imperiosis found by Mr. Barnum Brown out west this year…in our time," Emmeline proclaimed proudly, pleased to be displaying her knowledge of the ancient creature.

"And how do you know this?" Victoria asked skeptically.

"Mr. Brown is an assistant curator at the American Museum of Natural History back home. His fossil discovery has been all the rage…it's been written about in every New York and national newspaper!" Emmeline responded enthusiastically.

"You and your museums," Victoria responded, rolling her eyes.

"Welcome to the Duncan Theater! Can I help you with tickets?" called an older man standing behind a glass case filled with candy. They all turned to look at him, Lorna's eyes widening in pleasure at the popcorn happily bursting open in the commercial-size popper behind the counter.

"No, thank you, Sir," Stefan responded politely, speaking for the group. "We came in to get out of the rain. We're waiting for it to pass before we walk…home."

"My name's Tom…I like that better than sir," he smiled. "I think it's going to be a while before the storm passes. You might as well enjoy the movie while you're waiting it out," he said cheerfully, eyeing the old-fashioned clothes they'd donned for the Early American Days Festival. *They definitely get an A for effort,* he thought to himself.

"A moving picture?" Emmeline asked breathlessly.

Tom laughed. "I haven't heard a movie called that for a while, but yes, a moving picture. Jurassic Park is playing right now."

"A moving picture about a park?" Victoria questioned, feeling as if that would make for a very boring viewing experience.

"You've never seen Jurassic Park? Well, it's about a special park…a park with dinosaurs…like that Tyrannosaurus rex there," Tom responded, pointing to the large cut out they'd been discussing.

"Oh, that's a Dynamosaurus imperious," Emmeline responded knowingly.

"No, it's a Tyrannosaurus rex," Tom answered, smiling. "Check it out online when you get home…and the movie talks about it being a T-rex, too. Are you sure you don't want to see it? It's pretty awesome!" he said enthusiastically.

"We don't have any money with us, Sir…I mean, Tom,"

Stefan responded apologetically.

Tom paused, considering. "I'll tell you what…the movie has already started, so just go on in and enjoy it!"

"Oh, we couldn't impose," Emmeline objected.

"It's fine…no worries…enjoy!" he said, sweeping his hand toward the doors that led to the theater.

They looked at each other silently, their expressions uncertain. Finally, Victoria said decisively, "Let's do it!" and marched toward the double doors, the others following obediently behind her.

"Thank you!" Emmeline called to Tom over her shoulder.

"No problem!" he answered, chuckling at the very strange, but very nice kids.

As they walked into the dark theater, they immediately covered their ears as the booming crashes from the sound system shook the room. Their eyes were drawn to the huge movie screen, mesmerized by the images racing across it. They watched in terror as a red and tan Jeep careened wildly down a muddy road, the words *Jurassic Park* emblazoned on its doors. Two men and a woman inside the mud-spattered vehicle were screaming at the top of their lungs, their eyes crazed with fear. The gigantic dinosaur pictured out in the lobby was now fully alive and chasing the people, its deafening, ear-splitting roars filling the theater. The dinosaur craned its neck forward, reaching for the men and the woman, its razor-sharp teeth inches from tearing into their flesh. The beast burst through the remains of an enormous tree that had fallen across the road and crashed its head into the side of the Jeep, then sounded its thunderous roar yet again. The screams of the four time travelers perfectly echoed those of the passengers inside the Jurassic Park Jeep as they ran from the movie theater into the stormy night, screaming the entire way up the lane to the treehouse.

CHAPTER FOURTEEN

The next day, they stood at the bottom of one-hundred-and-eight resplendent granite steps, gazing up at the majestic monument sitting regally at the top of a grass-covered hill in the city of Canton, Ohio. None of them stirred for several minutes, somber as they reflected on what had happened to bring such a great man to this place.

"Such a horrible shame. He was truly a wonderful president," Victoria said quietly.

"I wanted you all to see this before you try to go back to your time," Glenda added, slowly starting up the steps that led to the circular, domed mausoleum where President William McKinley, his wife, Ida, and their two daughters were entombed.

Halfway up, Emmeline stopped and pointed at the stately bronze statue of President McKinley. "Oh, look!" She rushed over to the towering statue and slowly began reading the words inscribed in the stone beneath it. The others joined her, reading along.

"This statue is a representation of President McKinley speaking at the Pan-American Exposition," Glenda explained. They all turned to look at her, their eyes wide with understanding.

"It's so strange to think it was only a year ago that we lost him...in our time," Stefan commented, his face lined with grief.

"And lost him while I was with you. I hated having to tell you it was going to happen," Emarie said sadly.

"Why are people running up and down the steps?" Lorna interrupted, unable to drag her eyes from the men and women's bare legs in their running shorts.

"They're exercising," Glenda responded. "It's great exercise to run up and down these steps."

"Taking exercise on the steps of a deceased president's monument? That's scandalous!" Victoria responded, thoroughly disgusted.

"In your time, maybe," Emarie said. "But times change. Just look at you...you wear shorts now," she laughed, pointing at Victoria's exposed legs.

Victoria blushed crimson, fighting the urge to cover her legs with her hands. "I thought I would enjoy the thrill of wearing shorts, but I feel so odd. I don't think I care for it."

"At least I have a dress on," Emmeline said. "It feels very strange without my corset and petticoats, but at least my legs are decently covered."

"Well, I don't mind these overall shorts at all," Lorna declared. "I feel as free as a bird!" They all burst out laughing, amused by Lorna's unfiltered thoughts about her new clothes.

"Come on," Glenda urged after she'd caught her breath, "Let's pay our respects to President McKinley." They climbed the multitude of steps in silence, pausing at the top as they faced the enormous bronze doors that led into the mausoleum. "When these doors were installed, they were the largest in the nation," Glenda informed them.

"They're remarkable," Stefan responded, eyeing the impressive craftsmanship.

Quietly, Glenda reached for the doors and opened them. They walked slowly into the inner chamber of the immense mausoleum, stopping just inside the doorway. They looked around, absorbing the power and grandeur of the rotunda, and the sadness that hung over it even now.

"Let us ever remember that our interest is in concord, not conflict, and that our real eminence rests in the victories of peace, not those of war," Emmeline quoted quietly, reading the words engraved along the circular ceiling in the domed vault.

Victoria's eyes were immediately drawn to the two marble coffins sitting on a granite pedestal in the middle of the majestic room. "There he lays," she said, her throat tight with sorrow.

"Yes," Glenda said very softly. After several moments she pointed up, drawing their attention to the red, white and blue skylight at the very top of the dome. "The skylight has forty-five stars in the design to represent the forty-five states that were part of the United States at the time of President McKinley's death."

"At the time? There are more states in the Union now?" Stefan asked.

"Yes," Emarie smiled. "There are fifty states now."

"What are the names of the new states?" Lorna asked.

"Well, let me think…New Mexico and Arizona, I believe," Glenda answered somewhat unsure.

"Yes…and Alaska and Hawaii," Emarie chimed in, remembering her geography quizzing from school.

"That leaves one more," Victoria said, smiling slyly.

Glenda and Emarie thought hard. "It's Oklahoma!" Emarie exclaimed, her voice echoing loudly through the chamber. People turned and looked at her disapprovingly, shaking their heads. "Oops," she muttered, blushing.

"I think it's time to go," Glenda laughed.

"Just one moment," Emmeline responded. She walked slowly over to where President McKinley and his wife lay in the quietness of death and stood at the base of the marble pillar that held the two sarcophagi of William and Ida McKinley. "Thank you for serving our country," she whispered, tears brimming in her dark eyes. She turned then and rejoined the others and they made their way out of the magnificent resting place, slowly making their way back down the one-hundred-and-eight steps in complete silence.

At the bottom of the steps, Glenda turned to the four time travelers. "It's time now for you to try and go back. I hate to see you go since we're just getting to know each other, but your father needs your help."

"What if it doesn't work? What if we can't get back?" Emmeline fretted.

"I believe we'll be sent back," Victoria responded confidently. "We know we were sent here for a reason. That reason must have been to find out that father *was* found to be innocent of attacking the guard. We know now that someone very cunning framed him for that hideous crime. I believe it's our mission to go back and find that person and expose them," she said, her jaw set with determination. "And to see father freed!"

"We're going to get him!" Lorna shouted, pumping her fist in the air.

"You do beat all, child!" Glenda chuckled.

"I don't beat anything! I'm not wicked!" Lorna protested, her eyes blazing with defiance. For the second time that day, they all burst out laughing at one of Lorna's comical comments.

"It bothers me that I'm never going to know how you find out who did it," Emarie said sadly after the laughter had faded to amused smiles. "...or ever know why the person who actually committed the crime was never revealed. I just don't understand why that information was withheld from the public in 1902."

"Perhaps…perhaps we'll find some way to let you know," Victoria ventured.

"I just don't see how," Emarie questioned.

"That's why life is so interesting," Glenda responded to Emarie. "You never know what it will bring. Did you ever think you'd travel through time? Did you ever think you'd see your friends again after you left them? But you *did* travel through time and you *have* seen your friends again. If it's meant for you to know what happened with Mr. Hill, then you'll know," Glenda concluded, her wrinkled face shining with wisdom.

Emarie, Victoria, Emmeline, Lorna and Stefan all looked at one another – then smiles spread across their faces as the hope of possibility dawned on them. Instinctually, they moved closer together and joined hands in solidarity, the golden September sun shining down on their friendship.

Glenda looked on, tears wetting her eyes. "Well, let's get to it and see what happens. I have a gut feeling that you kids are going home today."

CHAPTER FIFTEEN

Glenda turned the key in the lock and pushed the door open. She stepped inside and held it while the anxious young people who were on the brink of the unknown filed in. The air in the antique shop stirred with their entrance and the distant past seemed to settle on their heads, welcoming them.

"So, this is Arnold's Antique Shop...where it all started," Victoria said dreamily, her eyes traveling over every nook and cranny of the store.

"It's a magical place. I can feel it in my bones," Emmeline added in a hushed voice.

Lorna ran her fingers over the stack of old books just inside the doorway, then picked one up, examining it closely. "Look!" she exclaimed. "This book was printed in 1900!"

Stefan peered over her shoulder, reading the copyright

information. "Extraordinary!" he breathed softly.

"This is my favorite place in Killbuck…or probably anywhere," Emarie told them. "I don't know why…but because the past is safe here, it makes me feel safe, too."

"Do you know…what you just said is actually very profound," Glenda said, softly touching Emarie's cheek. "I love you, dear child."

Emarie smiled and reached up, laying her hand over Glenda's. "I love you, too."

"Okay, let's do this," Glenda said after several seconds of fighting back tears. She led them to the work bench in the back of the store where the Underwood No. 5 sat waiting expectantly.

Victoria rushed up to it, bending down to scrutinize the brass plate on the side of the typewriter. "It's true! This *is* our typewriter!" she exclaimed excitedly. *"Property of the Hill Wallpaper Co.,"* she read out loud.

Emmeline, Stefan and Lorna joined her, staring at the Underwood. "It's hard to believe," Emmeline said, her voice hushed in awe as she reached out, lightly touching the typewriter.

"Are you ready to try?" Emarie said, her heart beating hard.

"Yes, we're ready," Victoria said resolutely, nodding her head.

"You need to change back into your clothes from home for the typewriter to work," Emarie reminded them, pointing toward the restroom near the back of the store. All of your clothes are in the restroom. Go ahead and change and then we'll get started."

Twenty minutes later, they were all back in their clothes from 1902 and ready to be transported back in time to fight for Brandon Hill's freedom.

"Can I ask something first…before we try?" Emmeline asked Glenda and Emarie, wringing her hands.

"What is it?" Glenda asked.

"Well…our lives…what happens to us…who we marry…when we…when we die…you would know all of that from looking at your computer here in the future. I would like to know. Can you tell us about our lives before we leave to go back to our time?" Emmeline asked.

Glenda looked at Emmeline tenderly, her life-worn face lined with concern. She tugged on a grey curl, deep in thought for several moments. Finally, she spoke, her words gentle. "I understand your curiosity, Emmeline. If I were a time traveler and had a chance to know my future, I would want to know, too. But it's not a wise thing to do…to look into your own future. It would make you afraid…it would make you question all your choices…a sense of doom would fall over your life. No…we weren't meant to live that way, my dear. We were meant to live without looking over our shoulder every minute, waiting for what we know is going to happen. It would ruin your life. Trust that I'm right about this."

Emmeline looked into Glenda's eyes for several long moments, then slowly nodded her head, accepting Glenda's words. "I understand. I would like to know, but I acknowledge the wisdom of what you're saying. Thank you for your honesty," she said, gently squeezing Glenda's hands.

"Okay…are we ready?" Emarie finally said, taking a deep breath. Her heart raced anxiously, and she found it difficult to breathe. "I hate saying good-bye to you again, but I know that you need to get back to help your father."

"If the typewriter will let us," Lorna interjected, eyeing the Underwood with concern.

"Who should try to type?" Victoria asked, looking at

Emmeline, Stefan and Lorna.

"That reminds me!" Emarie exclaimed. "How did it work when the typewriter transported you here? Did you each have to type on it and you were sent one at a time, or did only one person have to type for all of you to be sent together?"

"Victoria tried it first and it didn't work, then Emmeline tried it with no success, then I attempted it and…nothing. It was Lorna typing on the Underwood that got us all through the portal together," Stefan explained.

"So, it took all of you at once?" Emarie questioned, fascinated.

"Yes, all of us at once!" Lorna responded enthusiastically.

"And what did you see in the cloud before you were transported?" Emarie probed, growing more excited.

"We saw exactly what you saw the day you left us in 1901…all of our faces in the clouds, but nothing else."

"You didn't see any other people or places in the cloud?" Emarie asked.

"No, just our faces," Emmeline replied.

"Hmmm...that's interesting," Emarie responded, pondering what they'd told her.

"I think it's time," Glenda gently interrupted, anxious yet impatient to see the wonder of time travel before her very eyes.

Victoria took a deep breath and looked at Lorna with a steady gaze. "Well," she said, sweeping her hand toward the Underwood No. 5. "You should try first since it worked for you last time."

Lorna gulped and walked toward the typewriter hesitantly, her hands beginning to sweat. She sat down in the swivel chair in front of the Underwood, staring at the gold letters that spelled out the Underwood name on the black metal of the typewriter and the piece of paper that was already in place in the typewriter's roller. She reached out ever so slowly as the girls embraced one another while Stefan and Glenda stood close to them, looking on. They barely breathed as Lorna stretched out her arms, her fingers making contact with the typewriter keys. She pressed firmly, waiting for the buzzing in her fingertips that would signal the beginning of their transport back to 1902. Nothing. No buzzing. No sensation at all. She turned and looked at them, her eyes wide with alarm. "It's not working!" she cried.

"We need to keep trying…one at a time," Emmeline encouraged, not willing to give up hope. "I'll go next," she volunteered. Lorna stood up and stepped away from the typewriter and Emmeline took her place, sliding into the swivel chair. She arranged the skirts of her dress neatly around her and then reached out with trembling hands, pushing her fingers down on the keys. Instantly, she felt the rush of energy surging through her fingertips, jolting her from head to toe. "It's working!" she yelled jubilantly. She immediately began typing the words that had now become so memorable for all of them: WHAT IN THE WORLD IS CAUSING THIS FEELING?

The swivel chair began rocking back and forth wildly, and Emmeline was barely able to keep from falling to the floor as an immense rush of wind filled the antique shop with a roar. Glenda screamed and clung to Emarie, her grey curls whipping against her face. The white, billowing clouds appeared as the wind blew itself into a frenzy, causing books and antique knick-knacks to fall from their shelves, crashing to the floor. They gasped in terror as they looked up into the cloud and saw a black-cloaked figure in the distance holding a noose. And then Victoria, Emmeline, Stefan and Lorna saw themselves running, chasing a man whose face could not be seen. To their amazement, Robert's face suddenly appeared, looking confused, but ecstatically happy. And lastly, Emarie appeared in the cloud, dressed in her shorts and t-shirt, running blindly down a dark alley as she looked over her shoulder in fear.

In the next second, Glenda felt Emarie being torn from her arms and pulled into the spinning vortex that had suddenly formed out of the violent wind. One by one, Victoria, Emmeline, Stefan and Lorna were drawn in next, rising into the furious cyclone. Glenda frantically screamed Emarie's name over and over as Emarie and the others were carried up and away, disappearing into nothingness.

CHAPTER SIXTEEN

Emarie struggled to open her eyes, fighting against the weight of her heavy eyelids. She slowly sat up, feeling around in the pitch dark she found herself in. Where was she? As the memory of the whirlwind snatching her away came flooding back, she called out into the darkness. "Victoria! Emmeline! Are you here?" She heard a low moaning in response and she turned in the direction of the sound.

"I'm here," Victoria yawned, sounding as if she were lying on the ground somewhere near Emarie's feet. "I don't understand why it's necessary for us to be put into such a deep sleep when we're sent through time."

"Where are we?" Emarie heard Emmeline's weak voice ask.

"Stefan, Lorna, are you here?" Emarie called again, reaching out into the gloom, feeling around on the ground.

"I'm here," Lorna groaned from somewhere nearby. As she opened her eyes, the black void terrified her. She scrambled onto her hands and knees, then rapidly crawled toward the sound of Emarie's voice. When Lorna reached her, Emarie pulled her in, hugging her tightly.

"Stefan?" Victoria called, sitting up.

"I'm here, I'm here," Stefan answered, his voice on edge. "Where are we?"

"I haven't the slightest idea...but it feels like a room," Victoria responded, touching what felt like a brick wall behind her.

"Why were we brought here? And, where are we?" Emmeline questioned.

"That appears to be the question of the hour," Victoria said sarcastically.

"Let me feel around," Stefan said. "All of you, sit close together while I try to figure out where we are." As Stefan rose to his feet, the girls talked to one another until they'd located each other. They held their breath as Stefan explored the room, fighting the urge to scream.

After several moments, they heard a rattling sound in the

distance. "What? What is it?" Emarie asked anxiously.

"It's a door, but it's locked," Stefan said, yanking and turning the doorknob. "It won't budge."

Lorna started to whine, her fingers digging into Emarie's arm. "Shhh, it's going to be alright," Emarie soothed.

"How in the world are we going to get out of here?" Victoria fumed. "We don't know where we are, what year we're in... nothing! This is ludicrous!"

"Shrieking your head off isn't going to solve anything," Emmeline admonished. "We need to keep our wits about us."

"Wait! I hear voices," Stefan said, pressing his ear to the door.

"Call to them!" Victoria shouted.

As Stefan opened his mouth to yell, Emmeline cut him off abruptly. "No, don't! We don't know where we are or who they are! They could be bad people! Listen first...see if you can tell what they're saying!"

Stefan pressed his ear against the door, struggling to hear through the thick wood. Several moments later he turned toward them, and though they couldn't see his face, his eyes were wide with disbelief. "You're not going to believe this," he said, dumbfounded.

"What is it?" Emarie whispered, filled with dread.

"I think…I'm not certain…but it sounds very much like Conrad Beesly's voice…and a woman…there's a woman with him."

"What?" Victoria hissed. "We must be in a room in the warehouse! Why would the Underwood deliver us right into the den of Beesly's thievery?!"

"I don't understand," Emmeline cried.

"And why was I brought here with you?" Emarie asked, finding it difficult to remain calm.

"There's always a reason," Stefan said, turning to address them in the darkness. "We know that by now. We'll find out why at some point. But for now, we need to figure out how to escape this room…but not until Beesly and the woman are gone. Keep your voices low. If he finds us, there's no telling what he'll do to us."

"The snake should never have been released from prison!" Lorna seethed.

"He only spent a few weeks in prison for falsely accusing us of stealing 'his' carriage when you were here last year," Emmeline explained to Emarie. "No matter how much Senora Sierra raged about his thefts in the neighborhood, it couldn't be proven."

"Your father was very upset with Captain Claus about us ending up in jail and even complained to the mayor about it…how did Beesly get off so easily?"

"There was no real evidence, so there was nothing that could be done to keep him there. Father was quite furious about it," Victoria whispered.

"Shhh…he's coming closer," Stefan said.

They held their breath, waiting silently in the darkness. They clearly heard the evil cackle of Conrad Beesly's laugh as he passed by on the other side of the door. Emarie stifled a scream as Lorna's fingers dug deeper into the flesh of her arms. The next thing they heard was a woman's tinkling laughter.

"Who in the world is with him?" Emmeline whispered. "She has a fancy laugh."

"A fancy laugh?" Emarie questioned quietly.

"Well, she laughs very politely…as if she's a society woman. Why would a society woman be keeping company with the likes of Conrad Beesly?"

"Please…quiet," Stefan urged once again. He pressed his ear

tightly against the door, straining to hear every word that passed between Beesly and the woman. After several minutes, he turned back toward the girls who were sitting perfectly still in the inky blackness of the room. "I can't believe it," he said in a dazed voice. "I simply cannot believe it."

"What? What are they saying?" Victoria pressed, rising to her feet.

"They're planning a robbery," Stefan answered, his voice low.

"A robbery!" Emmeline shrieked, then covered her mouth in horror as her cry echoed loudly in the room.

"A woman…possibly a society woman…planning a robbery?" Victoria exclaimed. "How can it be?"

"Where? Who? Who are they planning to rob?" Emarie asked.

"A jeweler on Madison Avenue," Stefan answered, still bewildered.

"What?!" Victoria hissed a second time. "Robbing a jeweler? That's madness!"

"It sounds as if they've done it before…as if it's

commonplace for them," Stefan said. "They were talking about how to distract the guard…what to do if he spotted them…they said they would…"

"Hurt him?" Emmeline asked, fear in her voice.

"Yes," Stefan said softly.

An uneasy hush fell over them before Emarie broke the silence several moments later, asking Victoria and Emmeline a question that sent chills down their already terrified spines. "Do you think…is it possible…that Beesly and this woman did the same thing to your father…tried to rob his store and when the guard caught them in the act…they attacked him…and then made it look as if your father did it?"

CHAPTER SEVENTEEN

Emarie heard Emmeline gasp in the darkness. "Could it be? Could that actually be what happened?" Emmeline questioned.

"It would explain why the typewriter brought us here to Beesly's warehouse!" Victoria added.

"Yes! That *must* be the reason!" Emarie agreed.

"But if it's true, how will we know for certain and how will we prove it?" Lorna asked in a hushed whisper.

"The only way we can discover the truth is by first getting out of here," Stefan interjected.

"And how are we going to do that?" Victoria asked.

"Feel around…see if you can find anything we could use to break this doorknob off," Stefan answered.

The girls began to crawl on their hands and knees, feeling around on the floor and running their hands along the brick walls of the room. A minute later, Lorna called out in a loud whisper, "I think I've found something!" As if she were blind, she tried to decipher the object in her hands, running her fingers along every inch of it. "I think it's a shovel," she said excitedly.

"Bring it here…follow the sound of my voice," Stefan said.

Little by little, in the complete darkness, Lorna inched forward with the shovel in her hand. At last, she made it to Stefan's side and handed it to him, exhaling a sigh of relief.

"Is it safe to try and break the doorknob off right now?" Victoria asked from a far corner of the room, her words tinged with worry.

"I don't hear them anymore. Everything is quiet. Get ready," Stefan said.

They held their breath as he felt for the doorknob and then positioned the head of the shovel directly above it, bringing it crashing down onto the knob with the full force of his strength. The girls cringed in the darkness, praying that Beesly and his feminine cohort wouldn't hear the noise.

"It's loose," Stefan said, shaking the damaged knob. "One more blow should do the job." For a second time, he raised the shovel and brought it crashing down on the doorknob. In the next second, they heard it clatter to the ground, spinning until it finally settled limply on the ground. Stefan jammed his fingers into the empty space and pushed, knocking out the knob on the other side of the door. He then slid the latch bolt, and the door gave, creaking open. A shaft of light filtered into the room, causing them to squint as their eyes adjusted to the brightness.

He cautiously stepped forward and stood in the corner of the doorway, looking left and right for any sign of Conrad Beesly. The warehouse was quiet and still. "Let's go," he said, signaling to the girls to follow him. They crept forward slowly, their hearts pounding in their chests. They made their way through the dusty warehouse, tip toeing around piles of broken-down carriages, old trunks, piles of old books and empty whiskey barrels. They moved in complete silence, afraid to utter a single word for fear they would be discovered.

When they had almost made it to the front entrance of the warehouse, they suddenly heard voices behind them. Stefan turned and looked back at the girls, his eyes wide with fear. He quickly scanned the room, then silently pointed to a tall pile of old whiskey barrels stacked haphazardly near a wall. They ran for the barrels as quickly as their feet would carry them, barely making it behind the ramshackle fortress before the voices of Beesly and the unknown woman were upon them.

"My dear, you are simply a goddess of deceit," they heard Beesly say, a self-satisfied chuckle gurgling in his throat.

"Why, thank you," the woman responded, her delicate laugh echoing through the immense warehouse.

"Who would ever guess that Gwendolyn Fox, wife of the heir to the Fox fortune, is a conniving and cunning thief?" he cackled.

"Who indeed?" Gwendolyn smiled, her eyes glinting with triumph. "I told Damian that I could never be satisfied with the boring life of a New York socialite, but he wouldn't listen. He insisted on marrying me...essentially bought me from my father by offering him money for my hand in marriage. He'll rue the day he sentenced me to a life of boredom," Gwendolyn drawled, daintily clasping her gloved hands together.

"Yes, he certainly will!" Beesly laughed uproariously.

"When will we make our move on Darius Jewelers?" Gwendolyn asked, her haughty voice as smooth as silk.

"I want you to go in first and find out all you can about the layout of the shop and the schedules of Mr. Darius and the rest of his staff. I'm sure he sees wealthy women in need of another bauble every single day…he'll never suspect a thing. You can go in multiple times in search of the perfect necklace or ring and ask 'innocent' questions about the store and how it operates. This needs to be planned perfectly before we attempt it. This will be our biggest hit yet," Beesly said smugly, brushing back a strand of dark, oiled hair that had fallen onto his forehead.

"It will be our crowning jewel…pardon the pun," Gwendolyn laughed, immensely pleased with herself.

As they talked, Emarie carefully positioned herself between two barrels where there was just enough space to make out Beesly and Gwendolyn Fox a mere foot from where they stood. Her eyes widened in surprise as she gazed upon the elegant and extraordinarily beautiful Mrs. Fox. She was impeccably dressed in a gorgeous magenta gown, her head dramatically decorated with a jeweled and feathered hat resting upon shining, upswept brunette hair. *How could someone so wealthy and beautiful turn to a life of crime for fun?* Emarie wondered to herself. She looked at Victoria beside her, and shook her head in disbelief, her eyes conveying the astonishment she felt.

"Let's just hope we don't run into the same trouble we ran into when we attempted to rob the Hill Wallpaper Company," Beesly said sarcastically.

"Yes, nearly killing a man wasn't part of the plan…but he made it unavoidable by stumbling upon us," Gwendolyn said dismissively. "Thank goodness you hit him from behind. If he wakes up, there's still no way Hill can get off. We've thought of everything," she said smugly.

"Framing that snobbish rat was my coup d'etat," Beesly sneered. "He'll regret the day he ever had me kept in prison for weeks on end. I hope he hangs!"

Behind the whiskey barrels, the hateful words burned in their ears as they turned to look at each other, their eyes blazing with fury. Victoria moved forward, no longer caring about her personal safety, determined to confront the evil Conrad Beesly and his ruthless sidekick. Emarie grabbed her, holding her back. "No! No!" she whispered vehemently, as Victoria struggled against her hold, pulling away.

As Emarie lost her grasp on Victoria, they fell forward, and the wall of barrels came crashing down with a thunderous roar, exposing them to Beesly and Gwendolyn Fox. As if ice had suddenly fallen over the room, they all stood frozen in shock, eyeing one another, waiting for someone to make the first move.

CHAPTER EIGHTEEN

"You vile and despicable creature!" Victoria finally shouted at Beesly, her face beet-red with anger. "How dare you?! How *dare* you hurt an innocent person! And framing my father for *your* crime?! You should have been left to *rot* in that prison last year!"

Conrad Beesly sneered, his face contorted with disgust. "Do you think I'm afraid of the likes of you, you snooty little brat? I'll knock your head off, you self-righteous prig!" he yelled, lunging toward Victoria.

With a supremely elegant and controlled motion, Gwendolyn Fox reached out and placed her gloved hand on Conrad Beesly's chest, stopping him in his tracks. "Conrad, control yourself. These children are obviously over-wrought and wanting very badly for their father to be innocent...but he's not. Nothing they *think* they heard can change that," Gwendolyn finished, the hint of a smile on her lips.

Beesly caught on, joining in with Gwendolyn's manipulation. "Yes, you're right. It's so sad. They want their father to be innocent so they're making up stories and trying to pin the blame on us for something we never did."

"Shame! Shame on you!" Emarie erupted, wanting to punch Beesly.

"Child, now it's your turn to control yourself. Please stop screaming. And why are you traipsing about in your undergarments?" Gwendolyn asked, looking down her finely shaped nose at Emarie.

"That's none of your concern!" Stefan growled, his dark eyes flashing with anger.

Gwendolyn Fox sniffed, ignoring Stefan as if he were a dead bug on the floor of the warehouse.

"We're going straight to Captain Claus to tell him what you've done!" Emmeline exclaimed, pointing her finger at Beesly and Gwendolyn Fox.

"That's right! We'll not stand for this!" Lorna shouted.

To the outrage of the five young people standing before

them, Conrad Beesly burst out laughing at Lorna's display of childish fury and Gwendolyn laughed tinkly laugh, dismissing them completely.

Anger burned in Emarie's heart and before she could stop to think about the consequences, she shouted, "Do you know who *will* care about what we just overheard the two of you say? And who *literally* has an axe to grind with you, Beesly? Senora Sierra, that's who! I'm going to tell her right now and then we'll see who laughs last!"

Gwendolyn's eyes narrowed, and this time she didn't stop Beesly when he lunged for Emarie. Emarie screamed and took off running, adrenalin and youth giving her a head start on the hefty Conrad Beesly. Emarie ran straight for the warehouse doors that Senora Sierra had taken an axe to the last time she'd been in search of the sniveling Beesly. She threw open the doors and ran like the wind toward Senora Sierra's tea house, darting past ladies in their long gowns and men in their coats and top hats strolling down the New York City sidewalks. The women shrieked, thinking that a child in her underwear was on the loose, and the men shook their heads in disgusted disapproval, wondering what the world was

128

coming to.

After running for several blocks, Emarie veered off the sidewalk into a side alley, hoping to throw Beesly off her trail. The daylight was instantly cut off by the tall brick buildings on each side of her. She felt as if her lungs would explode when she looked over her shoulder to see if Beesly was on her heels. As she made eye contact with him at the entrance of the alley, she suddenly realized that she was living out the vision she'd seen in the cloud as the portal had opened. The thought spurred her forward. Somehow, she knew that if she made it to the fierce and fiery Senora, the reason for this mad dash would be revealed. And she'd be safe. Senora Sierra had let Beesly have it once before and she could do it again – of that Emarie was certain.

She felt blisters breaking out on the back of her ankle as her sandal strap rubbed against it again and again as she ran. She tried to take in air but could barely breathe. Just a few more blocks and she'd be safe, but she didn't know how much longer she could go on. She heard Beesly scream at her. A hideous, evil bellow that let her know exactly what he'd do to her when he caught her. And then she heard shouting, and she looked back again, her eyes wild with fear and relief at the very same time. She saw Beesly strain forward

to try and grab her, but Stefan and the others were hot on his heels,

yelling threats at the thieving villain. Even as she ran, she was

struck with the knowledge that another one of the visions in the

cloud was coming to pass. Beesly had been the man chasing Emarie

in the vision in the cloud – and he was also the man Stefan and the

girls had been chasing. But what did it mean and where would it

lead? She remembered the black-cloaked figure with the noose in its

hand and hoped beyond hope that it didn't spell doom for any of

them.

She rounded the final corner before Senora Sierra's tea house

and somehow received an unearthly spurt of energy as she sprinted

for the door. She burst through it and fell in an exhausted heap on

the floor. She heard the one-of-a-kind shriek of the Senora and

knew she was finally safe.

"Emarie! Emarie, my child! What in the world is

happening? Why are you dressed this way?! Your hair! You look

as if you've been chased by a demon! Speak, my child! What has

happened?" the Senora demanded in her strong Spanish accent. The

patrons enjoying their tea and sweets watched in alarm as the Senora pummeled the disheveled Emarie with question after question.

All Emarie could manage to do was point at the glass door where Conrad Beesly loomed large on the other side, his black eyes boring into hers. Senora Sierra saw the wretched man and an animal-like growl like Emarie had never heard come from a human before erupted from deep in the Senora's throat.

"You!" the Senora screamed, loud enough to shatter the windows. She ran into the kitchen and emerged with what Emarie knew would be in her hands – her trusty axe. Senora Sierra ran for the door and at the sight of her, Conrad Beesly took off running just as Stefan and the girls arrived breathless on the sidewalk in front of the tea house. "Where? Where is he?!" she yelled, her axe held high.

Stefan reached out and laid his hand on the handle of the axe, lowering it carefully. "Let him go for now. We need your help. We overheard Beesly and a wealthy society woman talking about how Beesly attacked the guard at Mr. Hill's wallpaper store while they were trying to rob it – and then framed Mr. Hill for the attack. We need to find evidence that Beesly did it so Mr. Hill can be freed!" Victoria, Emmeline and Lorna looked on, watching as understanding dawned on Senora Sierra's pale face.

"That *vermin* committed the crime and is letting dear Mr. Hill pay for it?" she shouted, her dark eyes blazing fire. As Emarie joined them in the doorway, they all nodded vigorously, letting her know that Stefan's words were true. "I will help you! I will!" she swore, placing her hand over her heart.

"But how? How will we find any evidence that he did it? That *they* did it?" Emmeline asked.

"This woman you mentioned…you said Beesly was with a society woman? Who is she? What society woman would keep company with the likes of that snake?" Senora Sierra asked.

"Her name is Gwendolyn Fox and she steals for *fun*!" Lorna chimed in, disgust etched in her eleven-year-old features.

Senora Sierra's face went ashen as she stared at them in disbelief. "Mrs. Gwendolyn Fox?" she choked. After they all nodded, she spoke again, her voice barely a whisper. "She is one of the wealthiest women in New York City…in the country…and she steals for…*fun*?"

"Yes, she steals for fun…because she's *bored*," Victoria answered, her face flushed with anger.

Their eyes were trained on Senora Sierra's face as the seconds ticked by, watching as her stunned expression transformed into hardened resolve. "She likes fun, does she? Well, mark my words, children...we're going to show her some *fun*!"

CHAPTER NINETEEN

"Whoa!" Stefan called to the horses to bring them to a halt. He turned to look at the magnificent mansion towering above him, and immediately felt intimidated. "We've arrived," he called to the others inside the carriage.

Senora Sierra peeked out of the Landau window, a self-assured smile playing on her bright red lips. "Ah, Mrs. Gwendolyn Fox, are you ready for us?"

"I don't think the world is ready for you, let alone Mrs. Gwendolyn Fox," Victoria laughed. Emarie and Emmeline joined her in a fit of giggles while Senora Sierra watched them, arching a dark eyebrow in feigned outrage. "Let us go, girls," she said dryly after the giggles had subsided.

They each gathered their skirts and stepped out of the carriage one by one, collecting themselves before they walked into the unknown.

"You look like a proper lady again, Emarie," Lorna called from the bench seat of the carriage where she sat beside Stefan.

"And I feel like a proper lady, too," Emarie smiled, running her hands over the full skirt of the emerald green dress she now wore.

She'd been reunited with her lovely gowns yesterday after they'd hatched a plan with Senora Sierra to take down Beesly and Gwendolyn Fox, and then taken a horse-drawn cab back to the Hill's townhome. Praying their mother wouldn't catch them in the act, Victoria and Emmeline snuck Emarie in through the servant's entrance and up the back stairs to Emmeline's room where the clothes from Emarie's visit to 1901 were still tucked safely away in the bottom of a trunk in Emmeline's dressing room.

As far as their mother knew, Victoria and Emmeline were in the library where they'd been all morning – when in reality they'd left the house and gone to their father's offices with Stefan and Lorna and traveled through time to 2018 and then back to 1902 in an attempt to save their father from a horrible fate. While no time at all had passed for their mother, time had taken them on a journey one hundred and sixteen years into the future and back again.

After a restless night with none of them sleeping much, they were ready to put their plan into action. They told their mother that Emarie had come by for a visit after being away on a long tour of Europe with her family and that they were all going to pay a visit to someone important who might be able to help free their father.

Eva had risen from the dusty rose settee she'd been sitting on and gathered her daughters in her arms as tears spilled down her pale cheeks. Victoria and Emmeline sensed the words their mother wasn't saying. They knew she thought their effort was naïve and most likely futile. Eva Hill had fought with all her strength and resources to find the true culprit in the crime her husband was accused of, but with no success. The trap for Brandon Hill had been too tightly woven. She felt horrifyingly certain that her husband would not be coming back to them from the New York City prison known as The Tombs.

The girls now stood on the sidewalk beside Senora Sierra looking up at the stunningly beautiful Fox mansion gleaming in the sun, contemplating all that had happened and all that was to come. The Senora had become their ally in the attempt to save Brandon

Hill, but there were some secrets they had to keep even from her. If they were to tell her about their time travels, she'd run from them like men ran from the angry bulls in the Senora's native country of Spain. She'd be gone in an instant.

"Let us face our foe, young ladies. It is time," the Senora said somberly, her words breaking into their thoughts.

Together, they slowly walked up the long, terraced sidewalk leading up to the massive front doors of the Fox mansion. As they walked, their eyes scanned the gorgeous landscaping bursting with vivid fall flowers and shrubbery sculpted into unique artistic creations. There were also exquisite marble statues that had been placed throughout the flora and fauna. It was a gorgeous display and they wondered to themselves how such beautiful surroundings could house such a corrupt and evil heart within its midst.

At last, they made their way up the steps to the sweeping front porch to stand before the massive front doors. Senora Sierra reached up and firmly struck the door knocker against the metal plate. They waited several moments in anticipation before a tuxedoed butler opened the door, imperiously looking down on them.

"May I help you?" he said, his face set to show no expression.

"Yes. My card," Senora Sierra said, extending her calling card, placing it in the small silver tray the butler held out to her.

"Please, do step inside. I will see if Mrs. Fox is in," the butler responded stiffly.

They picked up their skirts and stepped over the threshold into the foyer of the magnificent home. The butler bowed and then strode off at an even pace. They stood dumfounded as they gazed at the grandeur surrounding them, their eyes sweeping high and low, taking in as many details as possible. Victoria and Emmeline knew what it was to be wealthy, but this display of wealth was beyond anything they could imagine possessing.

Two enormous teardrop chandeliers hung suspended from a ceiling twenty-feet high and sparkled gloriously in the afternoon sun flooding in through floor-length windows in the immense foyer. A majestic fountain that looked like it should have been in the courtyard of the Louvre stood between an imperial staircase that swept upward to the second floor from opposite sides of the entryway. The whole effect of the foyer was dizzying in its splendor and they couldn't imagine what architectural glories the rest of the house must hold.

The butler soon returned, breaking their reverie. "Mrs. Fox is not in this afternoon," he said in a flat, monotone voice.

Senora Sierra inhaled deeply, readying herself for battle. She looked at the butler evenly, her dark eyes glinting as she challenged him. "Please tell Mrs. Fox that we are acquaintances of her friend, Mr. Beesly. I'm sure she will want to see us," the Senora said confidently, not backing down.

"Very well," the dark-haired butler responded, turning on his heel and marching back to the interior of the resplendent home. He returned a few minutes later, his pace much quicker than the pace with which he'd left. "Mrs. Fox will see you now," he said, his cheeks dotted with color.

"Yes, I am sure she will," the Senora muttered under her breath as Emarie, Victoria and Emmeline huddled close to her.

They followed the butler deep into the bowels of the home and then stopped behind him before two mahogany doors. The butler swept the doors open and then stepped into the room, announcing their presence. "The Senora Sierra Amador-Andres and company," he said in a clear, strong voice.

After they entered the drawing room, the butler stepped backward a few steps, then took hold of the drawing room doors, closing them with a flourish as he exited the room. It took everything the girls had not to gasp aloud in wonder at the beautiful room that was covered in mauve, cream and pale blue floral patterns from floor to ceiling. It could easily have been gaudy, but it wasn't. It was the most impeccably styled and beautiful room any of them had ever seen.

Gwendolyn Fox stood rigid before a white marble fireplace, her back to them as if to signal her disdain for their presence there. After making them wait a full minute, she leisurely turned to face them, lifting her chin in defiance as her eyes bored into them with cold fury. "I'm going to speak very slowly so you understand," she began, her voice dripping with arrogance. "If it's money you want, money I will give you. Then, you will never return to this home. If you do, you will dearly regret it," she concluded, her lips lifting ever so slightly in a hard smile.

Victoria, Emmeline and Emarie joined hands as they stood next to Senora Sierra, trembling. But not the Senora. She lifted her chin to mimic the movement of Gwendolyn Fox and stared deep into the other woman's eyes to let her know that she had met her match. "My dear, surely you did not think it was going to be that easy. No, no, no…it is most definitely not going to be that easy. We have come to make you a deal. If you accept our offer, you will be free. If you do not…well…you will live in a prison of your own making for the rest of your life!"

CHAPTER TWENTY

Emarie gulped as Gwendolyn Fox stepped away from the fireplace and moved toward them with slow, deliberate steps. The skirts of her magnificent lavender gown swished along the floor, accentuating each step she took. The girls instinctually moved backward, but the Senora held her ground, not budging. Gwendolyn stopped within a foot of Senora Sierra and smiled, her bright white teeth shining between pale pink lips. The Senora smiled back and raised her chin ever so slightly, signaling to her adversary that she was not afraid.

"Would you care for tea?" Gwendolyn Fox asked unexpectedly, sweeping her hand toward the cream-colored settees and pale blue wingback chairs.

The girls looked at each other in confusion, not understanding what was happening. But the Senora knew what was happening. It was going to be a chess game. A game of cat and mouse. Their foe was going to try to stop them through charm and subtle intimidation. The Senora smiled to herself. If it was a game of cat and mouse Gwendolyn Fox wanted, it was a game of cat and mouse she would get. "Tea would be lovely," the Senora answered confidently, her Spanish accent making the words sound like music.

"Come, have a seat. I will ring for tea," Gwendolyn purred. She turned and led the way to the sitting area and took the lead by sitting first. She perched herself on the edge of the settee, her back ramrod straight. She reached for a bell on the small end table beside her and rang it loudly. Within seconds, the butler appeared in a side doorway of the drawing room carrying a silver tray with a beautiful china tea set adorned with delicate pink roses. A uniformed maid followed closely behind with another tiered tray full of bite-size sandwiches and pastries. They set the tea, sandwiches and sweets on the long knee-high white table between Mrs. Fox and her guests and exited quietly without uttering a word.

Gwendolyn lifted the tea pot and began pouring tea into each of the cups. She gracefully extended each saucer and cup as she filled them, never making eye contact with her guests as she did so.

"She's trying to throw us off," Emarie whispered to Victoria, who was watching Gwendolyn Fox carefully.

"Throw us off what? The roof?" Victoria whispered back, confused.

"I mean, she's trying to make us feel like we're not important. She's not looking at us at all," Emarie whispered as quietly as possible as Gwendolyn reached for the teapot to fill one last cup.

After Gwendolyn had handed the last cup of tea to Emmeline, she swept her hand toward the sugar bowl and pitcher of cream as well as the tiered stand full of refreshments. "Please, do help yourselves," she said tartly. She then lifted the teacup she was holding and began very delicately sipping the tea, her brilliant blue eyes now focused laser-like on Senora Sierra's face.

The Senora sipped her tea, holding Gwendolyn Fox's gaze, refusing to be intimidated.

Finally, Gwendolyn cleared her throat, setting her teacup gently down on the table in front of her, then folding her hands demurely in her lap. "The weather is quite lovely today," she commented. "It would be a shame to see it turn stormy."

Emarie squirmed in her seat, wishing she could slap Gwendolyn Fox right across the face. She knew what was going on. She knew this wicked woman was trying to scare them by implying that things could get "stormy" for them if they didn't leave her alone. Emarie could tell that Victoria sensed Mrs. Fox's meaning as well when Victoria squeezed her hand, trying to hold back her anger. The Senora had warned them to maintain their composure no matter what happened, and Victoria was desperately trying to control her temper.

"Oh, a little storm is nothing to fear…it soon passes," Senora Sierra challenged, her voice dripping sweetness.

"I must beg to differ, Senora. A little storm can soon turn into a violent episode, hurting many in its path. I'm always wary of a little storm," Gwendolyn Fox countered, her words heavy with meaning.

"I hadn't thought of you as someone who would be afraid of a storm, Mrs. Fox," the Senora responded, not backing down.

"You misunderstand me. I'm perfectly safe here. I have no cause to be afraid…but there are some who are less sheltered who have every reason to be afraid. I do fear for those people,"

Gwendolyn responded with false sweetness, her eyes glinting malice.

Emarie, Emmeline and Victoria glanced from one woman to the other, their tea cups shaking in their hands as the subtle war of words between the two women raged on. They hoped and prayed the Senora would come out of this war the victor. So much depended on it. For Victoria and Emmeline, the life of their father could depend on it – there was nothing more important now than this battle going on before their very eyes.

"There is the illusion of safety when a house is built very well…but a powerful enough storm can bring even the most well-built home tumbling down," Senora Sierra jabbed.

Two spots of red suddenly burned in Gwendolyn Fox's cheeks, exposing her fury against her will. "And what storm could possibly be strong enough to bring down a home such as the one *I* live in?" she seethed through clenched teeth.

Senora Sierra took a long sip of tea, then daintily set her teacup in the saucer. "Wellll," she responded, "if someone were to tell the owner of this house that a person inside was trying to destroy it, I believe the owner of this house would be very, *very* upset. Very

146

upset, indeed."

"Do you think the owner of this house would *ever* take the word of a near-penniless immigrant that someone inside his house is trying to destroy it?" Gwendolyn shot back nastily, narrowing her eyes.

The Senora slowly sat her teacup and saucer down on the table between them and folded her hands in her lap. She glanced over at the girls and winked, letting them know that all would be well. The girls watched Gwendolyn Fox and the rage brewing in her eyes and weren't at all convinced that this encounter would end well.

The Senora gave a slight cough and then met Gwendolyn Fox's gaze with an unflinching stare. "The time for riddles is over, Mrs. Fox," she said evenly. "As you said earlier, let me speak very clearly so that you understand. If you do not go to Captain Sebastian Claus and tell him that Conrad Beesly is the true culprit behind the attack on Mr. Hill's security guard, then we will expose you to your husband. We are extending mercy by giving you the opportunity to betray Beesly in order to save yourself. But if you do not tell Captain Claus that Beesly is the one who left that poor guard left for dead and framed Mr. Hill, then we will go to your husband and tell him all that we know about your life of crime. This is our offer to you and we will make it only once. Expose Beesly and save yourself."

Gwendolyn Fox began to laugh her delicate little laugh, filling the room with the sound of her disdain. "And you have convinced yourselves that my husband would believe you?" she said after she'd regained her composure.

Senora Sierra smiled slyly, ready to play her trump card. She paused dramatically and then began to speak. "Oh, I am sure he won't entirely believe me…but a part of him will…and that part that already distrusts you will make him watch you like a hawk from that moment on until your last day on this earth. Your freedom will be gone. You will be a prisoner of your own making. You will never have a moment's peace again where your husband's eyes are not upon your every movement."

They all watched in amazement as the reality of what the Senora was saying hit home to Gwendolyn Fox. She looked as if she'd been run through with a sword. She tried to hide the deep swallow she took as she gagged on her own fear. To have her every move watched by the husband she despised was a fate she considered worse than death. Finally, she spoke, her words measured. "I will do what you ask," she said simply, her eyes never leaving the Senora's.

With those words uttered, Senora Sierra stood up, brushing out the skirts of her dress as the girls followed suit, quivering from head to toe. "I am so glad to know that we understand one another. You have until tomorrow morning to go to Captain Claus with a story as to how you know it was Conrad Beesly who attacked the guard. If we have not received word by noon tomorrow that Mr. Hill is to be freed, then we will tell your husband all that we know about your thievery."

Gwendolyn Fox nodded without speaking, giving the impression that she was in full agreement with the Senora's demands. In reality, her mind was swirling with plans to forever rid herself of the Senora Sierra Amador-Andres and her filthy cohorts.

CHAPTER TWENTY-ONE

As the carriage bounced along the city road, Emarie, Victoria and Emmeline's triumphant squealing filled the inside of the Landau carriage. "Oh, my goodness, that was so awesome!" Emarie shrieked.

"You most decidedly put that woman in her place!" Victoria agreed, laughing.

"I was so nervous, but you were so brave! It was extraordinary!" Emmeline chimed in, sitting excitedly on the edge of the red velvet seat.

Senora Sierra shook her head, her lips pursed. "Do not get too excited, girls. Gwendolyn Fox will not give up easily. You can see in her eyes that she's a determined woman. We must be cautious."

The seriousness of what the Senora was saying immediately

150

quieted all the delighted squealing inside the carriage. "What do you think she's going to do?" Emarie asked.

"I don't know. But I do not trust her. We must be on our guard until she does what we have asked her to do."

"Should we go to Captain Claus now and tell him everything?" Victoria asked anxiously.

"No. As we discussed before, he will never believe that Gwendolyn Fox is taking part in burglaries with a man like Conrad Beesly...*never*. Because of her station in life, Captain Claus will believe her if she denies taking part in the robbery of your father's shop. In order for Captain Claus to believe it, the truth about Conrad Beesly attacking the guard must come from Mrs. Fox herself."

"But how will she convince him? A woman like her coming in contact with a man like Beesly? What is she going to say to protect herself yet expose Beesly as the culprit?" Victoria questioned.

The Senora shook her head again. "I do not know. But she has a creative mind. She will think of something. She can say she was on her way somewhere in her carriage and saw Beesly coming out of the factory at the time of the burglary and assault."

"But won't they wonder why she was out so late…and in an industrial neighborhood? And won't they wonder why it took her so long to speak up?" Emmeline asked.

"Captain Claus will not question such a powerful woman. He will take her at her word. As far as taking so long to speak out – she can say that she does not read newspapers and was not aware of the situation, but as she heard about it in conversation socially, she finally put the pieces together. Many women in high society do not read the newspapers. It will seem a logical explanation. If she follows our instructions, she will escape suspicion…and it will be enough to free your father," she said, directing her gaze at Victoria and Emmeline.

"Oh, I hope so!" Emmeline breathed.

"But you don't trust her, do you?" Emarie observed, watching Senora Sierra closely.

"No, I do not. We can hope for the best, but we must prepare for the worst. If she does not do what we ask, we *will* go to her husband…but in the meantime, we must be careful. I would not put it past her to try and harm us in some way."

"Do you really think she would do something so bold?"

Victoria questioned, her face lined with concern.

"I do. I can see it in her eyes."

The girls sat back in their seats, stunned as they absorbed the Senora's words, tentacles of fear wrapping around their hearts. They sat in shocked silence until the carriage came to a halt outside of Senora Sierra's tea house.

"Girls, I know you are afraid, but we must have courage! We must be smart, and we must have courage! Stay together. Be aware of your surroundings. Watch closely until we receive word that your father has been released. The days of these vermin stealing and harming people is coming to an end! One way or another, we will stop them!" she said, her dark eyes burning with resolve.

"Thank you for everything you've done to help us," Victoria said emotionally, grabbing the Senora's hands in her own. "Whatever the outcome, we will never forget what you did today!"

"We will make you proud," Emarie added with conviction. "We will be brave!"

The Senora smiled and the radiance of it spread across her face. "I know you will!" she declared before gathering her skirts and stepping out of the carriage. Once outside, she paused to look back at them, her heart filled with pride. The girls watched as she walked through the door of the tea house, in awe of the amazing Senora Sierra Amador-Andres.

"Where to?" Stefan called from the driver's seat.

"Home!" Victoria answered. The carriage immediately lurched forward, the horses soon in a steady gait as Stefan steered them through the city traffic.

Emarie peered out of the small window as they passed block after New York City block, drinking in the sights and sounds of 1902. The wonder of this magical world of the past overwhelmed her with emotion. She sighed, wishing that Glenda could see this glorious place. As she drank it all in, Emarie spotted a blonde-headed little boy in the distance on the sidewalk. He was carrying a large burlap sack over his shoulder, struggling under its weight. Emarie leaned out of the window, examining the familiar-looking boy more closely. She gasped in delight as she suddenly realized who it was. "Robert! It's Robert!" she shouted, referring to the young boy they had saved from the orphan train the previous year.

"Oh, Robert!" Emmeline exclaimed. "It's been several weeks since I've seen him!"

"You've stayed in touch with him?" Emarie asked, curious.

"Yes, we have. I'm teaching him to read. I go to his home twice a month to help him with his reading."

"And his mother?" Emarie asked, afraid to hear the answer.

Victoria shook her head sadly. "She passed away a few months after we saved him from the orphan train."

"Thank goodness he was able to spend time with her before she died. It must have meant the world to her to have that time with him when she thought she'd never see him again," Emarie said softly.

"It was why the typewriter sent you to us…to save him from being adopted when he already had parents. We're thankful every day that you fulfilled your mission!" Emmeline said sincerely.

Victoria leaned out of the carriage window and called to Stefan. "Robert is walking on the sidewalk across the street. Please pull up," she directed.

"Yes, Miss Victoria," Stefan replied, ably steering the horses to the opposite side of the road.

"Robert! Robert!" Emmeline shouted, leaning forward toward the window.

The small blonde boy turned at the sound of his name, his face lighting with excitement when he saw Emmeline. He stopped in his tracks, waving exuberantly. He spotted Emarie in the other window of the carriage and began running toward the Landau, struggling to reach them under the weight of the sack he was carrying. "Emarie! You're back!"

After they had come to a halt, the girls rushed out of the carriage, smiling at the sweet boy who had become so dear to them. Robert raced into their arms and they hugged him tightly, returning his affection.

Across the street, a luxurious carriage rolled to a stop, the woman inside closely watching the reunion of Robert with his friends. She leaned out of the window and spoke to her driver. "Just as soon as they're alone...get rid of them," Gwendolyn Fox said coldly, her words hard and emotionless.

"With pleasure!" Conrad Beesly said gleefully, rubbing his hands together with anticipation.

CHAPTER TWENTY-TWO

"I'm so happy you're back, Emarie! You were gone so long!" Robert exclaimed.

"Yes, umm…well…my family was in Europe…for-for a long time," Emarie stammered, hating the dishonesty.

"How have you been, Robert?" Emmeline asked, trying to find a way to change the subject.

"I've been well. How is your father?" he asked, his face tight with concern.

"He's still in prison, but we know he's innocent and we can finally prove it!" Victoria answered, her words steely with resolve.

"You can? That's wonderful!" Robert said excitedly.

"It's just a matter of time before he's free," Emmeline added confidently. Emarie nodded in agreement with Emmeline, smiling as she recalled Senora Sierra's masterful handling of Gwendolyn

Fox.

"Who did it?" Robert asked, his eyes wide with little-boy curiosity.

"Terrible, evil people!" Lorna called from the driver's seat of the carriage, her voice full of outrage.

Robert's eyes grew wider. "What people? Who are they?"

"There are two people responsible and one of them is a very important and wealthy woman. We're trying to get her to turn on the other person involved. If our plan works, Father will be freed soon!" Emmeline explained.

"But...why would a rich lady need to steal from your father's business...and...and...why would they attack that poor guard?" Robert asked, mystified.

"The rich lady steals for fun...because she's bored," Emarie explained.

Robert gasped in disbelief. "What?!"

"It seems beyond belief...but it's true. After committing the crime, they framed Father for the attack...they made it look as if he attacked the guard out of anger when he supposedly caught the guard stealing from him," Victoria responded.

Robert shook his head as if trying to clear invisible cobwebs that clouded his understanding. "But…but…why would someone do something like that to your father? He's so kind!"

"Because one of them is Conrad Beesly!" Emmeline growled.

Robert drew back as if he'd been struck in the face. "What?! That terrible, rotten snake of a man?!" he shouted.

"We heard him admit that that's why he robbed Mr. Hill…for revenge…for having him kept in prison after he falsely accused us last year…and when the guard at Mr. Hill's company caught Beesly and the woman robbing the store, Beesly attacked the man and then framed Mr. Hill for the attack," Emarie interjected.

"That's *wicked*!" Robert shouted again, incensed.

"It is! And that's why we're going to put a stop to it!" Victoria responded firmly, her face glowing with anger. As she uttered those words of defiance, a shriek from Lorna pierced the air, startling them all.

"It's her! She's watching us!" Lorna shouted urgently.

"Gwendolyn Fox?" Emarie questioned, her heart pounding.

Stefan turned his head quickly, his eyes scanning the area

across the street. "Yes, it's her...and Beesly! Hurry! Get in the carriage!" he commanded, lifting the horses' reins in readiness.

"Who is it? The bad people?" Robert cried.

"Yes, we have to go!" Emmeline said hurriedly. "Run home now! She saw you talking to us!"

"But where will you go? What if she follows you?" Robert asked in a rush, tears forming in his eyes.

Emmeline looked at Victoria and Emarie and then up at Stefan and Lorna. "What should we do? Where should we go?" she asked frantically.

"We're closer to the factory than we are to home. Let's go there! Everyone will be working at this time of day...they won't dare follow us in!" Victoria instructed.

"He has a pistol! He's pointing it at us!" Stefan yelled, eyeing Beesly in the driver's seat of the carriage directly across the road. "Hurry!"

"Go!" Emarie shouted, shooing Victoria and Emmeline toward the Landau's open door. Robert watched in stunned disbelief as the girls flung themselves into the carriage and hunkered down on the floor to avoid a direct shot by Conrad Beesly. His mouth hung open in shock, his heart pounding in terror. He turned and began to run, his feet barely touching the ground as he fled.

Stefan steered the horses into traffic, urging them forward at a fast trot. "Yah!" he commanded, pushing them to their limit in the city streets. "Go!"

Lorna looked behind them, watching as Beesly pulled Gwendolyn Fox's elegant carriage into the driving lane. "They're coming after us!"

"He's not going to shoot us in broad daylight! He'd be a fool!" Victoria said, hanging on as best she could as the carriage bumped along at top speed.

"But what if he *is* a fool?" Emmeline wailed, barely able to keep from falling to the floor as Stefan rounded a corner and the carriage wheels tipped.

"We're only a few blocks from the factory! We'll make it!" Victoria reassured them.

"Why are they taking such a risk? Someone will see them!" Emarie declared, craning her head out of the window to see if the Fox carriage was still following them.

"They're trying to intimidate us! Don't they realize we'll

never give up when it means Father's freedom? They can try all they want, but we're not giving up until Father is freed!" Victoria asserted loudly.

They groaned in unison seconds later when Stefan hit a pothole and the carriage sank into the hole with a thud and then sprang back up, causing Emarie to go airborne. She crashed into Victoria and Emmeline on the opposite seat and they landed in a heap on the floor of the carriage, struggling to untangle themselves from each other as the Landau careened wildly toward The Hill Wallpaper Company.

When the seven-story building came into view, Stefan yelled to them from the driver's seat. "They're hard on our heels! I'm going to pull up to the front door…get ready to jump out!"

"How are we supposed to do that?! I don't know where my arm is!" Victoria shrieked as she pulled her arm from underneath Emarie's bottom with a grunt.

The carriage came to a sudden and violent stop in front of The Hill Wallpaper Company. Emmeline screamed when her nose crashed into Victoria's skull and a geyser of blood immediately shot out of her nostrils.

Lorna jumped down from the driver's seat and opened the side door of the carriage. "Out! Out!" she screamed. The bewildered and bloodied girls staggered from the Landau and into the shop as Gwendolyn Fox's horses slid to a halt in a cloud of dust directly in front of Stefan. Conrad Beesly dropped the reins he'd been holding and laughed maniacally before pulling the silver pistol from his pocket, pointing it directly at Stefan's heart.

CHAPTER TWENTY-THREE

Stefan had only a split second to think and before he could process what the consequences would be, he bellowed, "Yah!" to the horses at the top of his lungs, driving them forward into the horses at the front of the Fox carriage. Beesly opened his mouth in horror as the horses charged and then became tangled with the other horses in a frenzy of pawing hooves and terrified neighing. In the confusion, Stefan jumped down from the bench seat and ran into the storefront of the Hill Wallpaper Company, gasping for breath as he locked the door of the shop behind him.

He turned and saw the girls standing in the middle of the ground floor retail shop, staring around them in disbelief, their mouths hanging open. They thought they we would be safe because the shop and factory would be filled with people, but there was no one in sight. It was empty. Completely empty.

164

"Where is everyone?" Victoria shouted, her heart pounding with fear.

"I don't understand – it's the middle of a work day – everyone should be here!" Emmeline added, distraught.

"Maybe they're having a meeting in the offices!" Emarie answered, hoping beyond hope that she was right.

"Let's go!" Stefan commanded, leading the way to the stairs that would take them to the second-floor offices. They rushed after him, flinching when they heard the glass of the front door being shattered by the butt of Conrad Beesly's gun.

"Oh, no!" Lorna wailed, stumbling and falling on the steps. Emarie turned back and helped her up, holding her hand the rest of the way as they bounded up the steps two at a time to the offices above.

They were completely breathless by the time they made it to the second floor. They threw open the door to the offices and sprinted in, looking around in astonishment. Not a single person was to be found. The protection in numbers they had counted on had somehow mysteriously evaporated.

"Where *is* everyone?" Stefan questioned in alarm.

"You really should read the papers," they heard Gwendolyn Fox's voice purr behind them. They turned as one to face her and Conrad Beesly standing in the doorway, her eyes shining with satisfaction, his with joyful malice. "If you had taken the time to read the papers this morning, you would know that a prayer vigil is being held at this very moment for the guard who was so ruthlessly attacked by your *father*," she said, looking pointedly at Victoria and Emmeline with not even a trace of remorse.

"You wicked woman!" Victoria hissed. "You know it was Beesly who attacked him, and you know it happened because you were trying to steal from my father's shop!"

"How could you do such a horrible thing?" Emarie cried, lunging forward. Stefan grabbed her by the arm, holding her back.

Gwendolyn Fox shrugged her shoulders casually, unfazed by their emotion. "It wasn't meant to happen, but what will be, will be."

Beesly snorted with laughter, keeping the gun trained on them. "I'll be glad when I don't have to hear another word come out of your sniveling mouths!" he snickered.

"And I'll be glad when I don't have to hear another word

come out of *your* sniveling mouth!" Lorna declared, stomping her foot.

Conrad Beesly threw back his head and laughed as if he'd never stop until Gwendolyn Fox nudged him with her elbow, immediately silencing him.

"This is what we're going to do," she drawled in a tone of command. "You are all going to very quietly exit the building and get into my carriage without causing a scene. Then, we are going to put an end to this game. Do you understand?" she asked, her eyes narrowing menacingly.

In the midst of Gwendolyn Fox's threats, an idea hit Emarie like a bolt of lightning, and she took several tiny steps backward while forming her plan. Then, like a flash, she ran for the Underwood No. 5 sitting on the desk in the middle of the room. She quickly pulled the chair out and sat down, laying her fingers on the keys of the typewriter. "Get us out of here! *Get us out of here*!" she begged, praying the typewriter would carry them away. She immediately felt the buzzing sensation in her fingers as jolts of energy ran up her arms. "It's working!" she screamed to Victoria, Emmeline, Stefan and Lorna as they looked on with excitement, immediately realizing what she was trying to do.

"What is she up to?" Gwendolyn Fox demanded to know, showing a hint of anxiety for the first time. Beesly looked confused and uncertain. The gun lowered slightly as he looked to Gwendolyn Fox for direction.

At just that moment, Robert suddenly appeared in the doorway of the offices gasping for breath, his hair wet with sweat. "Here they are!" he yelled over his shoulder. Captain Sebastian Claus emerged beside him within seconds, his face beet-red with exertion.

Emarie glanced over, her heart surging with relief as she realized that Robert had led Captain Claus to them after hearing them say that they were heading to the factory to escape the threat of Gwendolyn Fox and Conrad Beesly.

"What in the world is going on here?!" Captain Claus's voice boomed as he focused on the shining silver of Conrad Beesly's pistol, his outraged voice ringing off the walls of the offices. "Am I to believe the words of this boy – that you, Mrs. Fox, steal for *fun* and that Mr. Beesly attacked the guard while you were attempting to rob Mr. Hill's shop?!" But even as he asked the question, the gun pointed at the children told him all he needed to know. It was true –

Brandon Hill was innocent.

Before either Gwendolyn Fox or Conrad Beesly could utter a

word in response, a furious wind suddenly rushed through the

offices, sending papers flying in every direction. Immediately, huge,

billowing white clouds formed in the air and in the clouds,

Gwendolyn Fox and Conrad Beesly saw themselves, looking

bemused and alarmed.

"What is h-happening?" Gwendolyn Fox stammered, her

voice filled with barely-controlled panic.

Emarie looked up at the clouds as her fingers hummed with

energy, completely confused. She had hoped the typewriter would

take them away from the danger they'd been in moments before, but

there in the cloud were the faces of Gwendolyn Fox and Conrad

Beesly. What could it possibly mean?

Then, in the mist of the clouds, other faces slowly appeared,

first faint and then growing clearer. Emarie. Victoria. Emmeline.

Stefan. Lorna. And lastly, Robert. All together as they trudged

through New York City – but a New York City much different

looking than the one of 1902.

"What?" Emarie whispered hoarsely as the vortex she'd come to expect began forming – a powerful whirlwind of air thundering through the cavernous office. She heard Gwendolyn Fox scream as she was lifted from the floor and drawn into the vortex, desperately struggling against its terrifying power. Conrad Beesly was airborne a split-second later, his black, oiled hair standing straight on end as he was drawn into the vortex next, disappearing from sight as he futilely screamed for help.

Captain Claus's face drained of all color as he stood rooted in place, speechless. Robert's knees buckled, and he collapsed on the floor, nearly fainting from fear.

"Get ready!" Emarie shouted, knowing what was coming. The others knew as well and braced themselves, joining hands. More gently than Gwendolyn Fox and Beesly, they were lifted up and drawn into the massive swirling vortex. Robert was taken in last, clawing at the air in terror, searching for a way of escape.

Emarie fought to reach his hand and finally grabbed it, holding tight. "It's going to be alright," she shouted over the deafening noise of the whirlwind. "We'll be together!"

Captain Sebastian Claus stood watching, completely

dumbfounded by what he was witnessing. He struggled to form words in a mouth dry from shock and disbelief. "No one is *ever* going to believe this!" he choked as his words were drowned out by the roaring wind.

THE HISTORY WITHIN *MYSTERY IN TIME*:

The mansion that Emarie's pen pal mentions in her letter is real and you can tour it in Akron, Ohio. *Stan Hywet Hall* was commissioned to be built in 1912 by F.A. Seiberling, a co-founder of the The Goodyear Tire and Rubber Company. In 1957, F.A. Seiberling's children began a foundation to preserve and protect the home. It is now considered a historical house museum and is a National Historic Landmark and is on the U.S. National Register of Historic Places.

Emarie's hometown of Killbuck, Ohio is a real village in Ohio along the Killbuck Creek. It was incorporated as a town in 1882. During the 1820's, Killbuck Creek was a navigable stream. Produce, pelts and other town goods were sent down the Killbuck on flatboats to Coshocton, Ohio.

The Killbuck Valley Museum is indeed real, and for a small museum, has a wonderful variety of fossils, preserved animals and other historical relics from Killbuck and the surrounding area.

The Duncan Theater in Killbuck was built in 1940 and after closing in the 1990's, was reopened in 2013 after being remodeled by locals, Cory and Randy Miller.

As Emmeline told the concession worker at The Duncan Theatre, the first remains of what we now know as *Tyrannosaurus rex* were originally named *Dynamosaurus imperiosis*. The remains were discovered in Montana in 1902 by paleontologist Barnum Brown.

The McKinley Monument in Canton, Ohio, is the final resting place of the 25th President of the United States, William McKinley. The monument was completed in 1907 and is designed in the shape of a cross-hilted sword.

CHECK OUT THE NEXT ADVENTURE

OF THE *IN TIME* SERIES

AS EMARIE AND HER FRIENDS GO

BACK IN TIME!

Made in the USA
Middletown, DE
25 April 2024

53459095R00099